Irreparably

Broken

By H. D'Agostino

Lynette,
Always fight
back. Love,
Heather
D'Agostino

~1~

Irreparably Broken

H. D'Agostino

Cover design by Kari March at K23Designs

Photography: Kelsey Keeton of K Keeton Designs

Model: Grant Mroz and Tessi Conquest

ISBN: 978-0-9912075-9-6

Table of Contents

Chapter 1

Maddie

"Hi, my name is Madison," I waved my hand around at the group of strangers surrounding me. I'd never been to this group before, and I still wasn't sure about whether I would become a regular or not. It had been a long day at work, and this spot happen to be closer to where I was at the moment than my usual one.

"Hi Madison," the chorus of voices called as I slumped back into my chair. I twisted my hands together and sighed. When would I be to the point where I wouldn't need these meetings? When would I get to that place in my life that everyone kept promising was in my future? It had been five years now, and it seemed that I was never going to escape my past. Every time I thought I was rounding a corner, something would trigger a memory and send me stumbling back into the darkness.

oooooooooo

After listening to yet another stranger spill their guts to the room about their latest triumph or downfall, I blew out a breath. Maybe I could sneak out. Maybe I could skip just this once, and the dreams would stay away. I was exhausted after all. Whenever I was tired, the monsters of the past seemed to leave me alone. Who was I kidding…I knew deep down that as soon as my head hit the pillow I'd been battling Richard all over again.

"You're new," a young blonde bounced up beside me as the group leader was closing the meeting.

"Uh yeah, I guess," I muttered as I pulled myself to a standing position beside her. She was petite, and I stood a good head above her with my tall frame. I turned to head for the door, not really wanting to talk to anyone, but this girl had other plans as she bounced along beside me.

"You wanna grab a coffee or something?" she smiled at me. "I'm usually too worked up after one of these to go home."

"Maybe another time?" I begged as I draped my jacket over my arm. "I'm rather tired tonight."

"Sure...ok," she dropped her chin and began kicking her toe at the ground as she turned away from me.

I don't know why I felt bad for ditching this girl I didn't even know her, but my instincts told me she needed a friend. I sucked in a breath as I looked longingly at the door before glancing back at her. "I guess I could put off going home a little longer."

"Really?" she beamed up at me. "I just thought..." she trailed off.

"No, it's ok," I motioned towards the door for her to go ahead. "I'm Madison, by the way, but you can call me Maddie."

"Erin," she stuck her hand out. "I've been coming here awhile, but I've never seen anyone my age before."

"Really?" I followed her as she shoved open the heavy door, and we made our way out onto the busy streets of Boston.

"Yeah," she nodded as she led us around the corner to Cool Beans. "I mean don't get me wrong, I don't mind spending time with the older crowd, but I'm only thirty. I don't have much in common outside the group with a forty-five year old."

"I guess you're right," I heaved the door open and held it for us as she made her way in and up to the counter. "It's like that where I work," I shrugged. "My boss is younger than me, married, has kids...we only really have our job in common." I didn't want to tell Erin that everything Hannah had, and I wanted too. I longed for a family that loved me. A husband who would come home and wrap me in his arms, children running and squealing through the house. I wanted it all. I had thought that I'd get it with Richard, but I was sorely mistaken.

"What do want? My treat," Erin nudged my side bringing me back to the present.

"Just a house blend," I mumbled as I glanced around the small store. I'd never run into Richard on this side of town, but I was always hyper-vigilant when I was out.

"You ok?" Erin handed me my steaming cup as she turned and searched for a place for us to sit.

"Sure," I muttered as we sank down onto the plush cushions of a nearby sofa. "My ex doesn't live far from here. I don't like being in his neighborhood," I scanned my surroundings again before beginning to relax.

"You have a restraining order, right?" Erin sipped her coffee as she watched me fidget.

"Of course, but that doesn't always work," I sighed.

"I can't argue with that," she shook her head "That's why I moved all the way across the country."

"I'd do that if my family weren't here," I shrugged and leaned back into the couch. "My mom and sister are all I have. I can't leave them," I mumbled.

"So were you married or just dating," she watched me out of the corner of her eye.

"Excuse me?" I swallowed.

"The ex," she lifted a shoulder. "Were you married or just dating?" She sat back and watched me as if she was waiting for me to explode on her.

"That's a little personal don'tcha think?" I cocked my head to the side.

"Well…we're all at group for the same thing…I already know your secret, so why not confide in me. They say it's good to have someone to count on," she lifted a brow and sipped her coffee again.

"I just…" I shifted nervously. Could I spill my guts to a complete stranger? One that I'd just met less than twenty minutes ago? Could I tell her about the demons that haunted me?

"Come on," she pushed on my knee. "I'll tell you mine if you tell me yours."

"I don't know if I can," I swallowed.

"His name was Gavin," Erin began. "We were high school sweethearts. He was the sweetest boy I'd ever met until he'd start drinking. The first time he hit me, and he apologized and told me it would never happen again. I believed him, until it did happen again." She looked up at me as a tear ran down her cheek, "The last time he hit me, he broke my nose. That was two years ago. I packed and left that night." She wiped at her eyes before turning her gaze back to me, "Your turn."

I inhaled deeply before squeezing my eyes shut and going back to a time I wished was just a nightmare, and not my past.

"Madison!!!!" Richard's voice bellowed as he stormed in the house searching for me. I don't know what I'd done this time to set him off, but I knew if I didn't face the music now, it would be worse when he found me.

"In here," I called from the kitchen.

"What did I tell you about dinner?" he growled.

"It's almost ready," I took a few steps back away from him. "I made your favorite...see?" I pointed to the oven where a roast was cooking.

"I told you that I like to eat when I get home," he clenched his jaw. "What time do I get home Madison?"

"Five-thirty," I whispered.

"What was that?" he narrowed his eyes on me.

"Five-thirty, Sir," I took another step back.

"And what time is it now?" he voice dropped even deeper and more menacing.

"Five-thirty?" my lip began to tremble. "Rich..." I slowly began to creep towards the door to the dining room. "It only needs five more minutes...I thought I'd try to surprise you."

"I don't know how many times I've told you what I expect when it comes to dinner," he roared as he charged towards me. "I've said this at least a hundred times...WHEN I COME HOME, DINNER SHOULD BE ON THE TABLE!!!!"

Before I could duck and get out of his way, I felt his fist slam into the side of my face. I recoiled against the shooting pain that was radiating outward from my eye. I cupped my cheek and scrambled back away from him as he stood seething over me.

"See what you did?" he yelled. "This is all your fault! You made me do this! Why?" he moved closer as I crouched in the corner of our dining room. "Clean this mess up!" he demanded. "I'm going out," he turned, grabbed his coat, and stormed out the door like a charging bull.

"That night was only the first of many," I glanced up at where Erin was watching intently. "I always thought he would change, but he never did."

"We all think that," Erin sighed wistfully.

oooooooooo

The bell on the door to the coffee shop dinged alerting a new group of customers, and I jumped to crane my neck. No matter how hard I tried, I was always prepared to run into Richard. He'd broken his restraining order once before, but after I had pressed charges, he'd stayed away. I always wondered if he was plotting a way to get back at me though. It never mattered that he was the one with the problem. He always found a way to make it mine. I lived in constant fear of him. Fear that he'd attack me when I least expected. Fear that he'd show up at my office. Fear that I'd never find someone to love me the way I should be

~ 12 ~

loved. Fear that I was to remain in this state of in between for the rest of my life. I had often wondered if I was irreparably broken, and if I could ever be put back together.

"You ok," Erin placed her hand on my knee. "You seem to be off in another world.

"This is normal for me," I gave a half smile. "I can't seem to stay out of the past. Knowing that *he* could walk in the door at any minute has me on edge. His office is right around the corner."

"Can I ask you something then, and please don't take offense at this...why did you pick the meeting that you did?"

"My office is two blocks away," I bit my lip. "I usually go to the spot near my apartment, but I was in a rush tonight, and decided to catch this one."

"So you're not coming back then?" Erin frowned.

"Probably not," I muttered. "I can't handle this stress.

"Could you give me the address to your regular meeting spot? I'll switch," she grinned. "I don't have many friends here. I'd like to have you as one...that is if you're ok with that. I mean...how many people understand what we're going through?"

"Sure," I smiled. "I'd like that too."

I pulled out a scrap of paper and jotted down the address to the church that was down the block from my place. "Here...we meet on Wednesdays," I handed her the paper. "I hope you can make it."

"Thanks," she stuffed the paper in her purse and glanced at her watch. "Well... I better go. It's getting late."

"Yeah...I got an early day tomorrow, and a busy afternoon," I stood and tossed my cup into the trash nearby.

"What do you do?" Erin asked as we headed for the door.

"I'm a vet," I smiled a genuine smile. I loved my job, and talking about it always brought joy.

"Cool," she giggled. "I love pets."

"Me too," we stepped out on the street together. "Well, I'll see you next week," I called as we parted ways, and I headed towards my car. I knew I needed to get home and try to sleep. Not that I'd be able too, but I needed to try. Maybe my newfound friendship would help. Maybe not, only time would tell.

Chapter 2

Maddie

As the early morning light filtered through my bedroom window, I stretched and yawned. It had been another rough night, and I was not ready to start the day yet. Richard had dominated my dreams. The sheets that were twisted around my sweat-soaked body were proof that I'd spent most of the morning hours fighting the demons in my head. I sighed as I rolled to the side and climbed out of bed. After grabbing a towel, I made my way into the bathroom. Maybe a hot shower would help motivate me for the day.

While the hot water beat down on my shoulders, I pinched my eyes shut and groaned. My muscles ached from being so tense for so long. Sleep had never been restful for me, and even though I was away from him,

I spent most of my time in a perpetual state of high alert. It was as if I was always prepared for him to show up where ever I was, and I wanted to be ready.

When I stepped out of the shower and stood in front of the mirror, I swiped my forearm across it trying to remove the fog. As much as tried to ignore her, the girl that stared back at me laughed. She knew all the times that I'd tried to hide the bruises, the cuts, and all the signs that Richard left...she knew all my secrets, and she mocked me when I faced her. It still hurt when I looked at myself. I could still remember all the lies I told friends...family...coworkers...all the lies that tumbled out of my mouth to explain away all the so-called accidents.

I lifted my hand and let my index finger trail along the light scar on my jaw. It was only visible when I washed the makeup off my face. Normally I kept it hidden. As one of my first reminders of Richard and what he was capable of, I examined it on a daily basis. I asked myself often, who would want me like this? Who could love a woman who was so damaged and broken? Was there a man out there that I could trust? If I found one...could I let him in?

I blew out a breath and shook my head, "Maddie, and you are so messed up you'd be lucky to find anybody." I turned and tightened my grip on my towel as I made my way back into my bedroom. After drying off, I dressed in a pair scrubs, twisted my hair up into a messy knot on top of my head, and began the process of making myself presentable.

ooooooooo

Looking nice had never been a problem when I was younger. All through high school and through much of my college years, I was a normal girl. Not in the popular crowd, but not an outcast either. I ran more in the middle of the pack. I was five foot five inches with long brown hair. I always had thought I was rather plain, but when Richard had noticed me, I began to see myself differently.

I had been sitting under a tree on the quad at school when he came up at plopped down beside me. "I didn't know they let girls into Harvard," he glanced at me and gave an amused smile. I wasn't one to let a guy crack a joke at my expense, so I shrugged as I retorted with, "Yeah they do, but you might want to hurry home to mommy so you can watch cartoons while you finish your homework."

"Ouch," he placed his hand over his heart and crinkled his nose. "I'm Richard," he held his hand out to me to shake and I gripped it firmly.

"Madison, but you can call me Maddie," I smiled.

"Ok Madison," he shifted himself so he could sit beside me. "Mind sharing the shade? I've got some studying of my own to do."

I furrowed my brow in confusion at him using my given name, but quickly recovered when he sank down beside me and pressed his muscled frame into the tree trunk... "Not at all," I moved over to give him some space.

"Thanks," he grinned at me as he pulled a binder from his backpack.

"What are you studying?" I craned my neck to see if I could read what was written on the top of his notebook.

"Criminal Justice. I'm going to be a lawyer," he lifted a highlighter and began marking up the pages before turning towards me, "You?"

"I want to be a veterinarian, but I've got to get into vet school first. Just basic classes right now," I held up an English Lit book as I rolled my eyes. "My mom wanted me to come to school here. It's just her now, so I figured I could do this for a little while before transferring."

"You doing anything later tonight," his eyes twinkled as he cocked his head to the side.

The tone of his voice set off warning flags, but the look in his eyes made me ignore them. I'd been at Harvard for a year, and no guy had ever approached me. I had begun to wonder if I was just that undesirable.

"No, nothing but me and the books," I shrugged.

"Wanna grab dinner with me? I mean…if you're not busy with the books, and all."

"Sure," I grinned. "Dinner sounds nice. I live in Hawthorn," began shoving items that I'd sprawled around me back into my bag. I knew if I was going on a date I needed to get back to the dorms and get ready.

"Where are you going?" he glanced up as I stood.

"Home," I bit my lip.

"So…seven? Does that work for you?" he placed his binder beside himself and stood.

"Sure…seven is great. I'll see you later," I smiled as I walked away.

If I'd known then what I know now, I would have run as fast as I could in the other direction as soon as he had sat down with me. Things didn't start off bad, but they never do. This type person…they find a way to insert themselves into your life at every turn. I didn't know it then, but by telling him where I lived…he made sure he knew everything about me.

oooooooooo

"Who was that you were talking to?" Richard wrapped his fingers around my arm and squeezed it tightly.

"We have Chem Lab together," I narrowed my eyes at him. "He wanted to study later."

"What did you tell him?" his fingers tightened even more.

"Owe, you're hurting me," I whimpered as I tried to pull away. "I wasn't doing anything."

"You're my girlfriend Madison. Nobody else gets time alone with you…do you understand me?" he growled as he leaned in close to my ear.

I nodded as I felt his hot breath on my neck. He paused a few moments before pressing a kiss to my temple. "That's what I thought," he released his grip on my arm and moved to stand in front of me. "Give me your phone," he held his hand out as an annoyed look spread across his face.

"Why?" I shifted my backpack around and reached in as I searched for my Iphone.

"I saw you with him," his voice was ominous. "Give me the phone."

Knowing that I hadn't done anything wrong, I placed the phone in his hand and rolled my eyes. "Go ahead," I shrugged and began to walk away. "I'm not cheating on you." I knew I shouldn't have mouthed off, but he was being ridiculous, and at the moment I'd never seen his violent side. He'd raised his voice and grabbed me before, but I was too naive to think that he'd actually hit me.

"I saw him give you his number. I'm taking care of that shit. You're mine, not his," he growled as his flicked his finger across the screen and pressed a few buttons. "Here," he handed it back to me.

When I brought the phone back to life, I noticed that Richard had cleared out its memory. "How am I supposed to study? I don't have any of those numbers memorized," I placed my hands on my hips and glared at him.

"You can study with me," he crossed his arms over his chest. "I don't want any other guys spending time with you. They want you Madison. They're not in it to study. They're in it to get into your pants. I'm the only one that's getting in," he leaned closer and kissed me. At first I was so worked up that I didn't respond, but as his tongue swiped across my lower lip, I

~ 21 ~

softened for him. "I love you Madison," he murmured. "Why do you always try to push me so hard?"

"I don't know…I'm sorry. I love you too Richard," I leaned into him as he wrapped his arms around my shoulders and began walking me back to the dorms.

ooooooooo

"I was such an idiot," I muttered as I was finishing up putting the final touches on my makeup. I tossed my compact back in the bathroom drawer and breezed back into the bedroom. After digging my shoes out of the closet, I slipped my ID badge over my head, grabbed my keys, and headed out the door. I knew just by the exhausted state that I was in that it was going to be a long day.

As I drove through town, I breathed a sigh of relief that I had such an understanding boss. Hannah Montgomery was a godsend. She was younger than me but wise beyond her years. She'd interned at New England Animal Hospital when she was in college, and once Dr. Henderson had retired, Hannah had taken over the practice. When I had searched for a job five years ago, Hannah had just been getting the practice going again. It was like the two of us were meant for each other. We worked well together, and while Hannah enjoyed taking care of the larger animals, I concentrated on the smaller ones. The only real secret we had between us was Richard. Hannah had been happily married to her husband Matt for eight years now, and had tried numerous times to set me up with friends. I had been successful so far in avoiding them, and I think Hannah had finally given up. She hadn't approached me in over six months, and I was hoping to keep it that way. Erin had been right the night before when she had said that normal people didn't understand us.

Most girls say that if I guy ever hurt them, they would go running in the other direction. I'm telling you, EVERYONE says that. I mean everyone. It's not as easy as it seems. Guys like Richard…they have a way of making you think that you're the one with the problem…that you're the one that's wrong. It took me being hospitalized to see that I needed to leave, and he's messed me up so bad on the inside that I don't think I'll ever trust anyone again. I want to fall in love, but I'm afraid. Afraid that I won't see the signs until it's too late. Afraid that men like Richard 'll only want me. Afraid that I'll be tricked again, and this time I might not be able to get away. What happens if I do find someone and they turnout to be dangerous?

"Knock, knock," a voice calls from outside my window causing me to jump.

I squeezed my eyes shut as my hand came up to press against my chest. "You scared the shit outta me."

"Sorry," Hannah grimaced. "Just wondering if you plan to come inside today. I've been watching you through that window for the last twenty minutes."

I sighed as I reached across the seat to grab my purse before climbing out of my car. I hadn't even realized that I had made it to work. I had been so lost in my head that I'd managed to park and turn the car off without even noticing. "I'm coming…I'm just tired," I mumbled as I stood.

"Well, I've got to head out to the Harris farm for the day. They're expecting a foal today. Think you can handle the office alone?" she smiled at me. "I can call Jenny in if you think you might need help."

"I'll be fine," I forced a smile back. I knew that once I got inside and started with my appointments that the craziness that was my past would subside and make way for the present. When I was in the zone, things seemed to run smoothly. As long as I stayed busy I didn't have to worry. "Go," I pointed to the truck was parked a few spaces down. "I'll see you tomorrow."

"All right...if you're sure," she studied me.

"I'm sure. I'll call in a vet tech if it gets too busy. Maybe I'll take lunch at the dog park today, that way I can do exercise time while I eat."

"Sounds like a plan," she called over her shoulder as she jogged off to the New England Animal Hospital work truck. "Maybe you can meet somebody while you're there."

I stiffened as her words hit me. Meet somebody? I was not hoping to meet somebody. Maybe I should call Jenny in, that way it could be her at the dog park, and not me. Yeah...I was definitely going to call Jenny.

Chapter 3

Maddie

As the hours ticked by, the office began to get more and more crowded. Clients that I hadn't seen in months all seemed to come in at once. The idea of handling all the appointments alone quickly flew out the window when the waiting area got to standing room only. After my third patient left I called Jo, our receptionist, in a room with me.

"Can you call Jenny, and maybe Ben in to help? It's crazy out there today, and I need to take lunch soon," I sighed as I shuffled some files around in front of me.

"Sure," Jo came over and began trying to help me with my burden. "You should take Zeb with you when you go out. I feel bad. He's been crated all day and needs to get out and exercise," she smiled at me as she headed back out to the waiting area to direct the next patient into the room.

Zeb was a rescue dog that lived at our office. Hannah had found him one day when she was returning from a client's farm. He was barely alive in a ditch alongside the road. I had taken an instant liking to him. He was a lot like me. You could tell by the way he whimpered and tried to cower in the corner of his crate that he'd been abused. Someone had mistreated this dog enough that it was terrified of humans. Over the last three months, I've spent every day working with Zeb, and trying to rehabilitate him. One day we're hoping he can be adopted out, but if that day ever comes I don't think I'll be able to let him go.

I'd take him home with me if I could, but my tiny apartment doesn't allow pets. If my landlord found out I had a dog, no telling what he'd do. Zeb wouldn't be easy to hide either. It's not like he's a little lap dog. No, Zeb is a one hundred pound German Shepard. He's a gentle giant I guess.

ooooooooo

By the time Ben arrived at the office, it was already past my lunchtime but I was taking my break. I'd decided that after Mrs. Simmons had come in with her Chihuahua saying it had swallowed a coin, at least that's what she thought, that I needed to get out of there or I was going to go nuts. My day had gone from busy to downright crazy. The only positive in being this busy was I didn't have time to dwell on anything but work.

"Hey Ben?" I called as I stuck my head out the door of the exam room. "Can you come in here a minute?"

"What's up Doc?" he grinned at me as he round the corner. Ben was a tall lanky kid. I say kid because he was only twenty-two. Ben had just graduated last May, and had decided to stay on with us. Hannah had hired him as an intern, and he was a great addition to our full-time staff.

"I really need to go to lunch. I haven't eaten anything yet today, and Zeb needs a walk. Do you think you could finish up with Mrs. Simmons? Sammy needs an x-ray to check for loose change," I rolled my eyes as Ben chuckled.

"Sure…anything for you Doc," he laughed as he reached for the chart in my hands and pushed the door open letting me pass in front of him.

"Thanks Ben, you're a life saver," I smiled at him and headed back to the kennel area to Zeb. "I'll be back in an hour. Call my cell if you guys need me for anything," I grabbed the leash, shoved my phone in my pocket, and grabbed the bag containing my lunch out of the fridge in our office before releasing the lock on Zeb's crate. He raced out and began bouncing on his hind legs as he tried to reach my face to lick me.

"Hey boy," I smiled at him and scratched behind his ears. "You wanna go for a walk? I thought we could go to the park, and let you run a little." Zeb bounced around as his tail beat wildly against the wall we were standing beside. "Come here," I cooed as a reached to clip the leash to his collar. Zeb ducked his head, and lowered himself to the ground by my feet. I don't know why he was always so gentle with me, but it was like he knew I was fragile, and we just understood one another. "All right," I grinned at him as the leash clicked in place. "Let's go!"

Once we stepped out of the office and into the bright sunlight, I couldn't help but sigh in relief. As much as I loved my job, being outside was a passion I'd had. If I could live outside, I would. Back in college I spent most of days on the quad studying that was the one thing that I fought Richard on the most. He'd started out requesting that I study at home. He claimed it was better that I be in the quiet of my dorm room. I didn't argue with him at first. He was older, and I figured he was just trying to help, but the more I stayed on the quad, the more he'd insist that I go inside. Now that I look back on it, I see he just wanted to control everything I did, and that was a way for him to hide me away from people. I never realized how isolated I truly was until I started going out again after I left him.

As the late spring breeze blew through the trees, I let Zeb lead me down the sidewalk. The dog park was only a mile away from the Animal Hospital, and Zeb knew the way without me leading him. We'd turned this trip into a routine a long time ago, and as long as I had help at work I was always able to make the trip.

"Are you in a hurry today?" I called to Zeb as he tugged on the leash. Normally I didn't have to worry about him dragging me down the street, but today seemed different. I guess maybe the fact that he'd been crated longer than usual was getting to him today. "Calm down buddy," I laughed as we made the final steps to the gate that housed his paradise.

Zeb began jumping when I stepped up beside him and released the latch. The dog park was fenced since it was in the center of several city blocks. It was like a small version of Central Park, only for dogs. Being off a leash was a treat for most city living dogs. The city had made this area special. Trees and benches were placed randomly, and a small pond was in the center. As long as your dog played well with others, it was a nice escape. Normally, I would come here at the end of the day, or first thing in the morning, but it had been so busy the last few days that my schedule was off. The few friends that I'd made here had regular routines, so I'd been sitting the last few days alone. "All right, sit!" I commanded as I closed the gate behind us as reached to unclasp the leash. Zeb lowered his hindquarters as I freed him. "Have fun," I scratched behind his ears before patting his side to let him know his was free to go. As he bounded away to join some of the other dogs, I looped the leash in my hand and made my way over to a bench in the shade. It was a rather warm day, and at the moment I wanted to relax and enjoy my lunch.

ooooooooo

Cole

I don't know how I got myself into this. Dog sitting? Who dog sits? When my sister had asked me for a favor, I had thought she's meant something easy like checking on Mom or something else equally responsible, but this? Not what I wanted to be doing on a Friday afternoon.

When I'd brought Banjo here on Monday, we'd had a nice time, He'd spent the day running around sniffing the other dogs, and I mean…I wish it were as easy for us men to search out women. Dogs had it easy. They walk up to each other, sniff each other's butts, and then either become best buds or enemies. I chuckled to myself as I thought about actually doing that to a woman. It would probably result in a slap to the face. I'd been slapped before, but I don't really remember why. When it comes to hitting on a woman, I'm usually at a bar or club, and I'm so drunk when it happens that I don't really remember what I've said. I just know they either slap me or come home with me. I've never worried about the ones that slap me. There's fewer of them, than there are of the ones that come home with me. I never thought of meeting someone here at the dog park, but after seeing her on Monday afternoon I've decided that I have to get her name.

This beautiful brunette came here on Monday, and I've been coming by here every day hoping to see her again. I don't know what it was about her, but I was drawn in. Her long brown hair was cascading down her back as she sat on a bench staring out into nothing in particular. I'd thought about approaching her, but she seemed lost in her thoughts. When I'd finally worked up the nerve on Tuesday, she hadn't shown.

I know…I know…I sound like a stalker, but I can't help it. I'm drawn her, and if she's here today…I'm going to get to know her.

oooooooooo

After freeing Banjo, I sauntered over to a nearby tree and leaned against it. I let my eyes scan the area looking for her, and when I found her, she was even more beautiful than I remembered. She was sitting on a bench about twenty feet away, munching on a sandwich and sipping a bottled water. Her hair was twisted upon her head, and the blue scrubs she was wearing were covered in what looked like cats of all different colors. Deciding that this was a sign, and I was going to talk to her today, I began heading in her direction.

oooooooooo

Maddie

I could feel it. A burning sensation crawling all over my skin. It started at the back of my neck and slowly spread to every part of my body. My nerves jumped to attention as my eyes began frantically scanning my surroundings. This was a feeling I got when someone was watching me. The first thought that popped into my head was Richard had found me. He had come into my neighborhood and was plotting away to get me alone. I'd never felt threatened in here before. There were always lots of people around which was comforting. In the past, Richard had liked to inflict his punishments in private. He always made sure that he caught me when he knew if I screamed no one would hear me. This feeling I was getting right now was causing that long suppressed fear slowly to consume me.

"Hi," came a male voice from behind me.

I jerked around to see the most beautiful chocolate eyes staring back at me. His hair was in that 'just got out of bed' style, and a small amount of scruff covered his jaw. "Hello?" it came out as more of a question than anything. I had no idea who this man was or what he wanted from me.

"Can I sit down?" he motioned at the spot beside me and rounded the bench.

As the words he'd just uttered rattled around in my brain, the fear I'd been feeling went into a full on panic attack. Those words...they were the same words Richard had used on the day we met. "No!" I forced it out as I stood and backed away from him. I scanned the park looking for Zeb. I wanted to get away from here as fast as I could. My fight or flight instinct was kicking in, and it was telling me to run.

This guy hadn't done anything, but the way he had snuck up on me, and the smug expression that he wore on his face told me he wasn't used to hearing the word 'no.' "I have to go," I mumbled as I watched confusion spread across his features.

"Can you at least tell me your name?" he lifted his arms as if he was trying to approach a wild animal.

"No," I shook my head before stepping back away from him. I crooked my fingers and brought them to my lips as I whistled for Zeb. When he came running, I quickly clipped the leash back in place and scurried for the gate. The dark stranger stood baffled in my wake as I ran, finally listening to my instincts, away from him. I had no intention of ever ignoring that feeling again no matter how attractive someone was.

Chapter 4

Cole

What just happened? I looked around to make sure I hadn't missed something. The way this woman jumped, and raced away from me would have made anyone question what I had done wrong. I've never in my life caused someone to run from me like that. I've seen anger that I've seen plenty of.

I settled down onto the bench she'd just vacated as I played what had just happened over and over in my head. Banjo seemed occupied in what he was doing, so I turned to try and catch a glimpse of her as she left. Who was she? Where was she rushing off to? And most importantly...what was her name?

Maddie

Breathe! Deep breaths! I pressed my palm to my chest and tried to slow my pounding heart. I don't know what's wrong with me. I've never fled a situation that fast before, and nothing about what had happened had been out of the ordinary. Whoever he was, he just seemed dangerous.

Ever had that feeling when you meet someone? That kinda feeling like they're hiding something? Whoever he was...he had that dark warning flashing over him. I'd missed it when I met Richard. I'd always told myself that I was worrying over nothing. All those times Richard would say or do something that didn't sit right with me. Every time, I would brush it away and tell myself I was overreacting. This time, I was going to listen. This time, there would be no chance of repeating past mistakes.

oooooooo

By the time I got back to the office, things had finally begun to slow down. Ben was filling out charts, and Jo was making reminder calls to the patients that had appointments for the next day.

"We've been talking about going out for drinks tonight at Vibe," he smiled over at me. "You wanna come?"

I stumbled slightly as I jerked myself to a stop, "You wanna go out with the boss?"

"Sure," Ben shrugged and then closed the folder he was writing in. He rounded the desk and began making his way over to me. He had a glint in his eye, and I could see all the signs plain as day on his face. "I think we could have a nice time."

"Ben," I sucked in a deep breath before blowing it out, I didn't want to make things weird or uncomfortable here at work, but Ben was too young for me. I was past that point in my life, and the fact that I was ten years his senior was glaringly obvious. "I don't think that's such a great idea. You're a nice guy, but..."

"I'm too young," he grumbled. "Age is just a number ya know?" he shrugged.

"Yeah, I know, but its a big number here," I grimaced as I watched his shoulders slump. "I'm sorry Ben. I'm just not looking for something right now."

"That's fine," he turned and slowly made his way back to our break room as he called over his shoulder, "I'll meet you there Jo. I wanna go home and shower first."

"Sounds good," she called before turning her eyes on me. "You know...I agree with you. He's too young, but you do need to come out with us sometime. You need to meet people."

"I'm perfectly happy with the way things are," the line had come out of my mouth so many times that I didn't even need to think about it anymore. "I've got a lot to do tonight."

"With who?" Jo's forehead wrinkled in confusion. "Everything around here is taken care of."

"Just some personal stuff," I glanced out the window of the office before heading to the front door to lock it. I really didn't want to give her any more information. I was planning to head to a meeting as soon as I escaped work. I knew that after my run in at the dog park with the dark stranger that I needed one. If I didn't get this off my chest, I was going to have a rough night sleeping.

"Well," she rolled her eyes as she braced herself against the counter "you have to promise me that the next time we go out after work you're going to come too. You docs have to cut loose too. Dr. Mills always go home to her family, and you go home to an empty apartment," she pointed her finger at me accusingly. "I know you do, so don't deny it."

"Fine," I grumbled "the next time you guys go out, I'm in."

"Don't make any plans for Friday night then," she grinned at me. "You're mine." She stood there for a minute smirking at me. She knew she'd gotten me, and she was waiting to see how I'd react.

"Whatever," I groaned. "Don't complain when I'm boring company," I warned as I turned to gather my things and head home.

ooooooooo

"So what's going on with you tonight?" Erin's shoulder bumped me as we left St. Matthew's and made our way to the parking lot.

"Nothing," I sighed as I clicked my key fob to unlock my doors. "It's just been a weird day."

"Like what?" she pressed as we came to a stop beside my little Honda Civic.

"I ran into someone today...sort of, and it's just put me on edge," I bit my lower lip nervously as I scanned my surroundings.

"Hey," she placed a hand on my forearm "whatever's got you so worried...you need to find a way to let it go."

"I don't know how," I dropped my eyes to the ground in front of me. "I thought I was past this," I rubbed my palm over my face. "It's just...this guy...it was something about him."

"Did you know him?" she moved around to the passenger side of my car and opened the door to climb in.

"No, and what are you doing?" I climbed in the driver's side and stared at her.

"You need to talk," she shrugged. "I'll get a cab from your place. It'll take the same amount of time for me to get home."

"Ooookay," I turned the key to crank the engine and began driving us the five blocks to my tiny apartment.

"About this guy," she smiled softly. "Did he say anything to you? Why do you think you need to be afraid of him? Do you know him?"

"Whoa!" I shook my head as I pulled the car into a parking spot. "No, I don't know him. I don't know why I was scared. You know how some people just give you that feeling about them? Well, I missed that with Richard. I don't ever trust people now...ever."

"So…how do ever plan to meet someone?" she wrinkled her forehead as she turned in the seat to stare at me.

"I don't," I turned off the engine and climbed out of the car. "I'm happy with the way things are."

"Liar! You are not," she shook her head and slammed the car door shut as she rounded the front of the car to face me. "You're scared every time I see you. You need to let that out. You're going to explode if you don't." She kicked at the ground before making eye contact with me once again. "What do you do to blow off steam?"

"What do you mean?" I cocked my head to the side.

"I mean…what do you do to let it all out? You obviously aren't with anybody right now. So it's not like you can vent at home."

I stood there for a few moments just letting what she said sink in. The therapist I'd gone to see years ago had said I should have a way to let it all out. She'd suggested running or going to the gym. I'd always been too busy to do any of that, but now…maybe I needed to reevaluate the situation.

Irreparably Broken- H. D'Agostino

"Earth to Maddie," Erin giggled as she nudged me. "Wanna come with me Saturday morning to work out?"

"Um, I guess," I blew out a breath. "I'm supposed to go out Friday night. I don't know if I'm going to be in any kind of shape to workout the next day."

"We can go later in the morning, and then have lunch," she smiled as she began digging in her purse. "Here," she handed me a business card. "My number's on the back. I workout at McKay's. It's about ten minutes that way," she pointed to the right. "Text me so I have your number, and then I'll send you directions on Saturday."

"Ok," I grumbled as I grabbed my cell and sent a quick 'hi' message to her. "I have to warn you...I'm not much of a gym rat. You might be shoveling me off the floor."

"I don't go all the time," she shrugged "but the punching bags will work wonders on your stress levels."

"Sure," I rolled my eyes at her. "I better be heading up," I swung my head in the direction of my apartment building just as a cab pulled up to the curb.

"All right...see you Saturday, and Maddie?" she called.

"Yeah?" I turned back in her direction.

"Not everyone's bad or dangerous. Not every man you meet is going to be like Richard," her smile was sad but held understanding.

"I know," I nodded before stepping through the door into my building. When I turned back around all I saw was the cab pulling away from the curb. I shifted my purse on my shoulder as I began climbing the stairs to my floor. I was tired today, but not tired enough. I knew as soon as I climbed into bed, I'd be transported back to Harvard, back to Richard, and back to the nightmare that plagued me.

Chapter 5

Maddie

After what felt like the longest work week of my life, it was finally the weekend. Friday was always my favorite day of the week. The animal hospital closed at lunch on Friday's and Zeb, and I would always take a long walk before I headed home for the weekend. Since Hannah had a large house, she took him home with her but our time was always special to me.

"So...you ready for tonight?" Jo leaned in my office where I was currently finishing up some paperwork for the day.

"What?" my head snapped up as tried to figure out what she was talking about.

"Duh," she rolled her eyes. "We're going out tonight, and you promised you'd come."

"Oh, uh...I guess," I shrugged as I rubbed my palm across my face. "I've got to finish this, so I might not be able to. I don't know if I'll have time."

"Whatever that is," she pointed to the paper in front of me "can wait until Monday. You're going, and that's final," she crossed her arms over her chest and began pouting.

"You're such a child," I grumbled as I shoved back from my desk.

"Only when I have to be," she laughed and then narrowed her eyes at me.

"Fine!" I snapped exasperatedly. "I'm coming. Are you happy now?"

"Very much so," she grinned. "Wear something nice to show off those legs of yours. We're going find you someone tonight if it's the last thing we do," she turned and began walking away as her laughter drifted down the hall.

"Wait! What?" I called after her, but she didn't respond. "Great," I thought as I turned back towards my desk and began packing up my things for the day. If I was really going to do this, I knew I needed to get home and prepare myself mentally for it. I hadn't been out with friends very often over the past several years, and whenever I did go out, I always had a hard time relaxing.

oooooooooo

After taking a long, hot shower, I now stood scrutinizing myself in front of the full length mirror on the back of my bedroom door. Even though it was spring, the evenings in Boston were still rather cool. After changing multiple times, I'd finally decided on a pair of skinny jeans and a loose top that hung off one shoulder. I'd always been told that I had nice legs, but I guess after all the times Richard had made me change my attire to something he liked, I now questioned everything. Tonight though, I was hoping to take back some control. The jeans fit me like a glove, accentuating every curve and dip of my body. They were a dark wash, and matched perfectly with the pale purple top I'd picked. My fair skin was just beginning to get that summer glow from all the days I'd spent my lunch break outdoors. My left shoulder peeked out of the neckline just enough to show a bit of skin. The cotton material draped on me in a 'Greek goddess' sort of way. I'd paired it with a deep purple bra since the strap would be on display.

I had no intention of attracting anyone tonight, but I felt good for the first time in a long time and wanted to show that off. I could always talk to someone tonight, right? Have a drink or two? I didn't look like I was trying too hard, did I? If a man did find my attractive, would he try to overstep his bounds? Was I asking for trouble? The questions kept coming the longer I stood there looking at myself. I'd gone from confidence to doubt faster than I thought possible. "Snap out of it Maddie," I scolded myself. Not wanting to talk myself out of this night of fun, I called for a cab and made my way down to the lobby of my apartment building. I knew I'd probably have a drink or two tonight, and I didn't want to worry about how I was getting home.

oooooooooo

When the cab pulled up to Vibe, I paid the cabbie and got out. I stood there for a minute on the sidewalk staring up at the sign. The bright blue neon shone in the dark like a beacon. The way patrons were walking up to the bouncer and forking over the $15 cover charge amazed me. I thought the place was pricey, but everyone else said it was worth it, so I came. Watching everyone amble toward the lights made me snicker. It looked like bugs flying into a bug zapper, blue light, and all. As I moved to get in line, the crowd seemed to grow and before long I was at the front. I showed the doorman my ID, like I didn't look twenty-one. I mean really...I'm thirty-one, but I guess I should feel good that I still look young, and pushed through the heavy door to enter the club.

Once inside I was surrounded by thumping music, and flashing lights of every color. It's funny, and I used to go to places like this all the time, but when Richard and I started dating he claimed that they were not his scene. I think the fact that I got hit on a lot whenever we would go to one is why he didn't like them. It was more of a need for control. Now that I was back in one, I couldn't help the feeling that swelled inside of me. It was as if I was throwing it in his face that I could do something he didn't approve of. "Take that Richard," I shouted as a broad grin spread across my face.

Before long I'd made my way to a corner booth where I found Jo and Ben along with Jo's boyfriend. Ben wasn't dating anyone regularly, but at the moment he had two girls sitting with him.

"Hey, you made it," Jo called as I approached.

"Yeah," I shouted back. It was a little quieter back near the booth they had chosen, but still loud enough that we had to yell to talk to one another.

"We need to get you a drink," she grinned as she pushed against her boyfriend so he'd let her out of the booth. "This is Ian, by the way," she motioned to the guy. "He doesn't bite, but he doesn't really talk much either," she grinned before leaning in next to him and placing a quick kiss to his cheek.

"Ha ha," he grumbled as he shifted to let her out. "Don't mind her," he glanced up at me. "She's had a few of these already," he lifted the glass of ice sitting on the table in front of him and waved it towards Jo.

"I see," I cocked my head to the side and sucked my lip into my mouth.

"Come on," she grabbed my hand and began dragging me behind her towards the bar.

After pushing through the growing crowd, we finally made our way across the room and to the long bar that ran the length of the opposite wall. There must have been a crowd three deep around the thing.

"What's with the crowd tonight?" I yelled over my shoulder as the group beside me jostled me.

"Friday is Ladies Night!" Jo shouted into my ear. "Drinks are half-price if you've got the goods."

"The goods?" I scrunched my nose up in confusion.

"Yeah, the goods," she grabbed her breasts and squeezed them.

"Jo!" I gasped as I shook my head.

"What? Sometimes being a girl is a good thing," she laughed and tossed her head back just as a group in front of us parted and allowed us to move up to the bar. "What do you want?"

"I don't know," I scanned the rows of liquor bottles that were lit up on the shelves behind the bar. "I'm not much of a drinker."

"That's a shame," came a deep voice from beside me.

I stiffened as every nerve ending inside me sprung to attention. This was it. A guy, no make that a hot guy, was hitting on me. I could see him out of the corner of my eye, and as he shifted to face me, I knew what was coming next.

"There's no way that a woman like you is here alone," his deep sexy voice poured over me coating me in a balm.

It was like he hypnotized me. I couldn't move or respond as I stared unabashedly at him. "Wh…what?" I stammered. Smooth, real smooth Maddie.

"I'm Cole," he smiled at me and cocked his head to the side.

Before I could answer, I stumbled forward from being pushed from behind. I reached out to grab the side of the bar just as Cole chuckled. "What the hell?" I glared over my shoulder at Jo.

"Tell him your name," she ground out as she leaned next to my ear. "He's hot," she winked, grabbed a drink that was placed in front of her, and then turned and walked away.

"Looks like your friend left you," he smiled at me again before shifting on his feet.

"What are you having?" the bartender broke the moment as she stood in front of me waiting for my order.

"Uh?" I nibbled on my lip as I scanned the liquor bottles once again.

"I'll take a Jack and Coke," Cole called out beside me. "Sorry," he grimaced when I looked up and him scowling. "It sounded like you needed more time."

When the bartender returned, I had finally decided on a vodka cran. When she handed me my drink, Cole tossed some bills on the bar shouting, "keep the change" before he turned back to stare at me.

"Where'd your friend go?" he scanned the area around us. "She's not a very good friend if she just walked off and left you with some strange guy hitting on you."

"We have a table," I swallowed as I looked away. I hadn't missed where he had mentioned that he was hitting on me. It had been so long since I'd actually flirted that I hadn't even been sure that it was actually happening, but he'd just confirmed it.

"What's your name?" he smiled again.

"I need to get back to my friends," I began to step away from him, but he reached out and wrapped his fingers around my arm.

"Please tell me your name," he leaned into my ear from behind me. "Don't runoff again."

I tried to swallow the tightness in my throat, "Again?"

"I saw you with your dog the other day," his grip tightened, and that was all it took.

I spun on him, fire in my eyes as the memories of Richard assailed me, "Don't touch me!" I recoiled away from him, and began backing up. As I took a few steps backwards, I tripped over someone behind me. Cole reached out and grabbed my hand just as my feet began to tangle with the girl behind me.

"Careful," he soothed as he wrapped his arms around me and placed me to the side of him. I stiffened, and he noticed. "I'm not a bad guy, really I'm not," he lifted his hands in front of himself in defense. "I just want to know your name."

I sighed before squeezing my eyes shut, and then turning to look into his, "It's Maddie. My name…it's Maddie." Before he could say anything else, I turned and scurried towards our booth as fast as I could through the crowd surrounding me. I only looked back once, and was shocked to see Mr. Tall, Dark, and Handsome staring at me. His dark eyes were burning holes in me as if he was entranced.

ooooooooo

Cole

It was her. I don't know how my luck changed from the shit day I'd been having, but as I made my way over to the bar…there, she was the girl from the dog park. When Wes had invited me to come with him tonight, I really hadn't wanted to. I was tired, and after my long day at the gym, all I wanted to do was have a couple of beers in the privacy of my home. He nagged me though until I'd finally agreed. Vibe was always jumping on Friday nights, and it was Ladies Night after all. I hadn't gotten laid in several weeks, and was hoping to find a warm body for the night.

As I pushed my way through the crowd, I watched her from behind. She was talking to the girl beside her, but I couldn't makeout what they were saying. She leaned into the bar, and I couldn't help but admire the view. Legs that went on for days were wrapped in dark denim that hugged her perfect ass. A light purple top draped loosely around her shoulders hiding what had to be perfect breast underneath. Her shoulder was peeking out of the neckline, and as she moved her chocolate hair swayed revealing her slim neck. God she was beautiful, and I felt like stalker as I watched her. Thinking that this would be the perfect girl to take home tonight, I sidled up beside her just as her friend asked her what she wanted.

"I don't know. I'm not much of a drinker," her voice was musical as she looked on with a confused expression.

"That's a shame," the words fell from lips before I could stop them. "Smooth Cole," I grumbled. She had me all kinds of twisted up.

"There's no way that a woman like you is here alone," I leaned closer so she'd know I was talking her. She had yet to acknowledge me, something I wasn't used to.

"Wh…what?" her voice hitched as she turned and stared at me. Her eyes were like saucers, round and wide. The darkness of the room prevented me of noting their color, but the emotion in them…that I could see. It was a mix between surprise and fear. I'm not sure why she would be afraid me, most women threw themselves at me. Surely with someone that was as attractive as she was, she would be used to getting hit on.

"I'm Cole," I held my hand out for her to shake, and waited patiently for her to respond. She stood there for a few moments completely lost in her own thoughts before her friend pushed her from behind. She scowled as she looked over her shoulder and snapped, "What the hell?" Her friend whispered something in her ear before slinking away, and leaving us. I grinned. I knew this move so well. I perfected it with my friends. Whoever this other girl was she wanted us to have time alone. Well, away from her anyway, we were hardly alone. "Looks like your friend left you," I cocked my head at her and waited for her to notice, but before she could respond the bartender interrupted us.

"What are you having?" the girl was clearly annoyed as she waited for our orders.

Deciding to put Miss Mystery out of her misery, I ordered first. "Jack and Coke." When the bartender returned with my drink and finished our order, I tossed a few bills on the bar and turned back to my beautiful companion. I was getting her name before she walked away this time, even if it killed me.

"Where'd your friend go?" I watched her to see if she'd even look knowing that this was my chance to see how interested she was in talking to me. "She's not a very good friend if she just walked off and left you with some strange guy hitting on you."

"We have a table," she swallowed and looked away. I couldn't really tell what it was, but she seemed so uptight and fearful of me that I wasn't really sure how to respond to her.

"What's your name?" I tried again.

"I need to get back to my friends," she began to step away from me, but I reached out and wrapped my fingers around her arm. I didn't want to watch her flee again, and it looked as if that was exactly what she was trying to do.

"Please tell me your name," I leaned into her ear from behind her. "Don't runoff again."

"Again?" her voice squeaked and sounded almost like a whimper.

"I saw you with your dog the other day," I tightened my grip as she tried to slip away, and she yanked her arm from me as if I'd burned her.

"Don't touch me!" she recoiled, and began backing up.

I watched her take a few steps backwards, and trip over someone behind her. I reached out and grabbed her hand just as her feet began to tangle with the girl behind her.

"Careful," I murmured as I wrapped my arms around her to steady her before placing her to the side of me. She stiffened, and narrowed her eyes at me. "I'm not a bad guy, really I'm not," I lifted my hands in front of me trying to show her that I was just helping. "I just want to know your name."

She sighed before squeezing her eyes shut as if this was the hardest thing for her to do, and then turned to look into mine, "It's Maddie. My name…it's Maddie." Before I could say anything else, she turned and scurried towards the back corner of the club as fast as she could through the crowd surrounding us. I couldn't help but stare as she was slowly swallowed up by the crowd. She was beautiful and delicate, not like my usual type at all. "Maddie," I rolled the name around in my mouth. At least I knew her name.

I turned to head back to where I'd left Wes only to find him laughing his ass off not ten feet behind me.

"Dude," he chuckled when I approached. "You got shot down!"

"Shut up!" I rolled my eyes at him.

"She was hot man...what'd you say to make her runaway like that?" he continued to laugh as I growled.

"Fuck you!" I shoved him as I tipped my head back letting the remaining drops of my drink slide down my throat. She was hot, and I had no intention of backing off. Maddie whoever she was was going to mine. I would find her again...after all...I saw her at the dog park before, I knew she'd be back. She'd come back, and I'd be ready. I'd make her mine. Sooner or later she'd give into me, and see that she was attracted to me as much as I was her.

Chapter 6

Maddie

By the time, I got back to our booth my entire body was shaking. The encounter I'd had with Mr. Dangerous had sent me into an adrenaline high. My brain had been screaming at me to get away, but at the same time it felt good to be noticed.

"So?" Jo looked up at me from her seated position and cocked a brow.

"So what?" I wrinkled my forehead as I sunk down on the cushioned bench of the booth.

"Who is he?" she rolled her eyes at me like I was the most exasperating person she had ever dealt with.

"I don't know," I shrugged as I muttered "some guy."

"Uh," she elbowed me sharply in the ribs.

"Owe!" I shifted away from her just as she tried to do it again.

"Well, whoever he is…he's staring at you so hard he might burn a hole in your head."

I snapped my head up and swung my eyes in the direction she was looking, and sure enough Cole whoever he was, had a heated gaze on me.

"He's hot," she smiled. "Why didn't you stay and talk to him?"

"I'm not looking to meet anyone right now," I blew out a breath and shook my slightly at her.

"Why the hell not?" she gasped. "I know you haven't dated anyone as long as I've known you, and I know that you have got to be tired of pleasuring yourself."

"Jo!" I hissed. "Shut up!"

"Oh, come on Maddie," Ben chuckled from across the table. "We know what you do when you're alone at night." His grin that he'd been sporting soon morphed into a look of pleasure as the girl that was sitting on his right shifted, and placed her hand between his legs

"You need to get a room," I grumbled as I felt my face heat. I knew Ben was a player, but I'd never seen him like this. It's amazing what a little alcohol can do to a person's inhibitions.

"Might just do that," he mumbled as the girl on his left began sucking on his neck. "Come on baby, let's get outta here," he shifted in his seat and began pushing the bimbos that were clinging to him out of his way. "Later," he called over his shoulder as he began walking away.

"Sure glad I didn't agree to go on a date with him," I shook my head at his antics as I glanced over at Jo.

"You have to remember he's in a different place in his life. He's younger than us," she shrugged as she tipped her glass to swirl the ice around in it.

"I guess," I muttered. I never got to experience that part of my life…Going out and casually meeting someone. I'd been so wrapped up in Richard that I'd completely skipped over the time to be young careless. Part of me wondered if I'd truly missed anything, and the other part berated me for even caring. I knew no one would understand. No one had in the past, and any new friends would see me as weak. Most people that found out about my past didn't understand. They would say that they did, but they didn't really. I mean seriously…who stays with someone that wants to control everything they do? Who stays with a man that hits them? Me, that's who…the old me that is. Now…I do everything I can to avoid ever going back there. I don't date, and I don't even really talk to men. When they do talk to me, I give as little information about myself as possible, hence the encounter I'd had tonight.

"Earth to Maddie," Jo shoved me lightly.

"Huh?" my head snapped to the side.

"I said we're taking off," Jo and Ian both began to stand, and Jo wobbled slightly. "I've got the morning shift tomorrow, and I need to get some sleep. Do you want to walk out together?"

"Sure," I swallowed the last of my drink, and quickly grabbed my purse to follow them to the front door. I knew I needed to call a cab, but I was thankful none the less that someone cared enough to make sure I got out of there ok.

oooooooooo

When morning came the next day, I groaned. The light shining in my room was way brighter than it needed to be. Thoughts of burrowing back down under the cover filled my head but were soon replaced by the sound of my cell ringing on my nightstand.

"Ugh," I grunted as I slapped around trying to make contact with it. "What?" I grumbled in the offending object.

"Good morning to you too," Erin's voice drifted through. "We're still on for the gym right?"

"The gym...oh crap!" I muttered. "What time is it?"

"Doesn't matter...I'm in the lobby. Do you want me to wait here or come up?" her voice was so happy and chipper that I wanted to scream.

"Give me ten minutes, and I'll be right down," I yawned.

"Ok, but if you're not down in ten...I'm coming up," the line went dead as another yawn escaped me, and I tossed the covers back.

When I shuffled into the bathroom, the dark rings around my eyes from last night's leftover makeup that I hadn't removed glared back at me. My hair was a tangled mess, and my eyes were bloodshot. "That's what you get, you dummy," I muttered as I reached for a brush. I shouldn't have gone out. Nothing good ever came from it.

After tying my hair back in a ponytail, washing the makeup from my face, and quickly dressing in some yoga pants and sports bra, I grabbed a water bottle and made my way downstairs.

"Took you long enough...oh shit, you look like hell!" Erin turned a concerned gaze on me.

"I'm fine...just a little hung-over. I went to Vibe last night with some friends," I sighed as I held the door open for us to head out onto the street.

"How was it?" she smiled softly at me. Erin knew what it was like to put yourself backout there after what I'd gone through. She was just like me in that aspect.

"It was fun actually," I opened her car door and climbed in. "Aside from some guy hitting on me, it was pretty uneventful."

"Some guy?" her brow raised as she slid into the driver's seat. "Was he at least hot?"

I nodded silently as I licked my suddenly dry lips, "Oh he was hot all right. Scorching hot."

"Really?" she grinned in my direction as she turned the key in the ignition. "Do tell."

"Everything you've ever thought of when you hear 'tall, dark, and handsome' this guy had."

"Come on...details girl...I need details," she giggled as she pulled the car out onto the street and began heading east.

"I don't know…I guess he was about six foot four maybe. I mean…I'm five five, and he dwarfed me. Dark hair…kinda messy. I couldn't tell about the eyes, but it was his mouth that I noticed the most. The most perfect full pink lips were surrounded by dark scruff." I shook my head as I tried to clear the image from my brain. I was not interested in this guy. I did not want to be involved with anyone, especially someone who looked like he did. He hadn't done anything yet, but the keyword was yet.

"Sounds delicious," she sighed beside me. "Next time you go out, you better call me. I need to meet someone."

"I don't intend on seeing him again. I don't know anything about him other than his name is Cole," I shrugged before turning to gaze out the window.

"You know," she paused as she turned into the parking lot of the gym and parked the car, "it's ok to feel something again. Not everyone's going to be like Richard."

"I can't take that chance," I mumbled. "I won't go through anything like that ever again."

"Well," she reached out and touched my arm causing me to look back in her direction "that's why we're here. We're going to learn how to kick butt."

"Huh?" I pushed open my door and climbed out of the car. "I thought we were just going to work out, and hit the punching bag a few times?"

"We are, but they teach self-defense here too. I signed us up for their Saturday class," she smiled at me as my mouth dropped open in shock. "I knew you wouldn't want to come," she barreled on as I stood there. "I thought it'd be good for us though. You'll thank me later."

"I tried self-defense when I was in school. It didn't work," I grumbled.

"I bet you didn't have a pro teaching the class," she giggled.

"What do you know that I don't?" I narrowed my eyes on her.

"Wes McKay...used to fight professionally," she chewed her lower lip as she watched me squirm. "He owns a gym and teaches the classes. He's been harassing me for a month to take a class."

"Wait, he knows about your past?" I watched her smile at me in satisfaction as I rounded the front of the car.

"Yeah," she lifted one arm and wrapped it around my shoulder. "He came to a meeting one night and offered his services to our group free of charge. He told some story about a friend of his growing up in a home with an abusive father. He said he wasn't able to help his friend back then, but he wanted to help break the cycle now," she squeezed my shoulders lightly as she led us to the door of the building. "He's a nice guy," she urged. "Just try it with me today, and if you don't like it, you don't have to come back.

"Ok, but I'm warning you…I'm not very coordinated," I groaned as we entered the gym, and I took in all the weights and various machines surrounding me.

ooooooooo

Cole

When my best friend Wes had asked me to help him with his self-defense class, I jumped at the chance. I mean what kinda guy would I be if I didn't find wrapping my arms around women while they rubbed against me a turn on? He hadn't bothered to tell me last night that the class was at ten o'clock in the morning. I know. I know…most of you must be shaking your head at me but when you stay out drinking all night…ten o'clock is early. Anyway…since I had to be at the gym early Saturday, I had opted to go ahead and try to get a morning workout in. I hadn't hit the weights in a couple of days, and I knew I'd feel the burn if I didn't get back to them soon. I'd just finished a run on the treadmill when I saw her walk in the door. Maddie…she was talking to another girl, a petite blonde as they made their way up to the front desk. What was the luck that the woman that I couldn't stop thinking about showed up here? Was the universe trying to tell me something?

After last night, I wasn't sure how I was going to go about finding her other than stalking the dog park, but here she was again, and this time on my turf. Wes was talking to them at the front desk, and they were nodding along, her friend a little more enthusiastically than her. Her friend giggled, and then they turned to head towards the room where we were holding the class. Was she in the class?

"Wipe the drool," Wes shoved me in the shoulder hard. I hadn't even seen him walk up to me I'd been so entranced by her.

"Shut up!" I scowled him.

"It's your mystery girl," he grinned. "But dude take it easy with her."

"What are you not telling me," I cocked my head to the side. "Is she married or something?"

"No…not married, but it's not my place to tell. Just trust me when I tell you to go easy," his eyes held a warning that I'd never seen him use before. It was almost like he was trying to pass a secret message to me. I didn't know what it might be, but after the way she ran from me in the park, and then last night…she practically bolted when I touched her. Now with the added warning from Wes, and the fact that this was a self-defense class…it was leaving me with a sick feeling in my gut. What was it that she was hiding, and why did I scare her so much? Did she have dark secrets like me? Was she just as broken? Knowing that I wasn't going to get the answers I so desperately wanted by just standing here, I grabbed my water bottle and a towel and slowly began walking towards the room we were having the class in.

Today I would back off. I would show her she could trust me. If her secrets were what I thought they might be, she was going to need a friend right now. She was going to need a protector, someone who would stand up for her, and if I had any say in it…it was going to be me.

Chapter 7

Maddie

Once Wes had directed us into the room in the back corner of the gym, I dropped my things in the corner and took a seat beside Erin. There were about six other women in the room at the moment, but I was sure there would be more. Sadly, there were always more. Other than the women in my group, my boss, Hannah, was the only person who knew my secret. Her sister and brother-in-law were both doctors, and they had told her that they saw people like me at the hospital all the time. I knew there were others, but I somehow always felt alone.

"Good morning ladies," Wes's voice was deep and rumbling when he walked into the room. "It's good to see all of you here today," he smiled and scanned the room. When his gaze landed on me, his eyes widened slightly. It was like seeing me was a surprise or something. I couldn't figure it out, I mean…he saw me walk in here. He talked to me. He knew I was here, but when his assistant ambled through the door it all made sense. "I have someone helping me out today," he motioned toward the door where Cole was standing. "This is a friend of mine…his name is Cole Walker. Cole meet the ladies," he grinned as Cole sauntered to the front of the room shaking his head.

As I watched them talk to each other in whispered tones, I turned towards Erin, "That's him."

"Him?" she wrinkled her nose at me.

"The guy from last night…that's him," I hissed as I felt a shiver run through me. Goose bumps erupted all over my body, and my senses went on high alert. It was as if my instincts were shouting DANGER at me.

"Yum," Erin giggled and wagged her brows.

"I gotta go," I turned to the side and began to stand just as Wes's head snapped up.

"Oh good, we have a volunteer," he smiled brightly at me as if he knew what I was trying to do.

"Uh no, you don't," I mumbled just as Erin wrapped her fingers around my wrist trying to halt my escape.

"Don't be shy," Wes coaxed. "Come here."

I could feel the blush spreading as I stood frozen in place. My brain was battling back and forth with whether I wanted to run like hell or stick it out.

"I..." I stammered as I let my eyes dart around. Everyone in the room was staring at me.

"Come here," he motioned again. "I promise...this escape is easy, and you get to teach Cole here a lesson," he grinned a toothy grin and winked at me.

I don't know what it was about him, but he was easy to be around. It was almost soothing the way he made me feel. It balanced out what I was battling inside myself being around Cole. I let my shoulders drop into a relaxed state as I began making my way to the front of the group.

When I reached him, I turned my back on Cole. The smug look on his face had caused anger to rise in me, and now the idea of teaching him a lesson sounded appealing.

"Ok," Wes moved to stand in front of me, whereas Cole moved behind me. "Today we're going to work on getting away The key to self-defense is not overtaking your attacker, but trying to avoid a situation in the first place." He leaned in to me and asked my name before continuing. "Maddie here is going to escape her assailant when he tries to grab her from behind."

My eyes went wide as the words echoed around the room. Grab me from behind? That did not sound like something I wanted to be a part of. It was as if Wes knew what I was thinking when he saw my face and made eye contact.

"Relax," he soothed. "I'm gonna walk you through it. You're safe here."

Even with his encouragement, my body stayed on high alert. It was like I was forcing myself to endure something that I knew I couldn't handle.

"Now," he faced me but directed his words to the group. "If you're ever out somewhere, and someone sneaks up behind you, the first thing you should do it yell 'No!' Then, you're going to swing your arm like this," he grabbed my wrist and pushed my arm back so I would make contact with Cole's nose. "When your assailant rears back to protect himself…that's your chance to escape. Most of the time whoever is holding you will release their hold to tend to themselves. If they don't…" he smirked. "You yell 'No!' again and," he bent down and grabbed my ankle "you step back and stomp on their foot." He looked up at me from his crouched position and grinned. "Wanna try it?"

I swallowed as I glanced back at where Cole was standing behind me, "I don't know."

"You can do this…I promise…and you won't hurt him," he assured me. "We're trained in this for a reason. We know when to let go, and how to get out of the way," he smiled again.

"Ok," I murmured.

"Just remember what I just said," he nodded and before I could blink, two strong arms wrapped around me from behind.

I froze as fear and memories assailed me. Richard's face came to the front, and my entire body went stiff leaving me standing there shaking. My arms and legs went stiff as I squeezed my eyes shut remembering the last time I was held like this…

"Madison!" Richard bellowed from the bedroom.

"Just a minute," I sobbed as I blotted the cool cloth against my split lip. I'd met some friends after class, and made the mistake of getting

dinner with them when we were finished. One of Richard's colleagues had seen us and told him. Now here I was trying to pull myself together before bed, hoping just to get through whatever wrath he had left for me.

"No! Now!" he shouted as he shoved open our bathroom door and barged in.

I stiffened as I watched his body fill the doorway before daring to make eye contact.

"Why do you do shit like this Madison? Why do you make me do this?" he came up behind me a trailed his knuckles along my bare arm.

"I'm sorry," I murmured. "I didn't mean to," I lowered my eyes to stare at the red-tinged water in the sink. "It's just Andrew…" I trailed off as I watched the rage that had begun to settle, fire backup again.

"Do you like him?" he boomed. "Do you want to fuck him?" he leaned right next to my ear and growled, "No one is gonna want you. You are a worthless excuse of a girlfriend. You don't know your place."

"I didn't mean…" I started to move away, but he pressed into my back pinning me against the counter.

He reached around and grabbed the washcloth out of my hand, and tossed it on the edge of the sink, "It's time you learned your place." He wrapped both arms around me from behind and spun us.

Richard was tall, and with my small frame I was no match for him. Fighting him only made him happy. It was like he took joy out of forcing me to do something I didn't want to do.

"I really don't feel like it tonight," I begged as he carried me toward our bed.

"I don't give a fuck what you feel like!" he tossed me on the mattress and leaned forward covering me with his body. "Take these off before I rip them," he growled into my ear before pressing a kiss to the side of my face.

That night had ended like many others, with me crying in the bathroom and thanking god that I was on birth control. Richard never used condoms, and I'm sure if I got pregnant he would have found a way to make it my fault.

ooooooooo

As Cole held me, I felt my body give out. It went limp, like it knew what was coming and that it was going lose the battle. After a few minute of nothing happening, Cole loosened his hold. His entire demeanor changed as his arms went slack.

I felt myself sag against him as if the encounter completely drained me. I hadn't exerted any energy, but my brain was telling my body that it couldn't compete with the wall of muscle behind me.

"Are you ok?" his voice was like warm caramel coating me.

I shook my head slightly embarrassed, "No...no I'm not."

Wes gave a slight nod as Cole placed both of his hands on my shoulders and began leading me back to my seat. He helped me sit down, and then handed me my water bottle.

I sat there in a daze for the rest of the class. Embarrassment, and frustration battling for the win in my head. Erin had given me a few understanding looks, but never said anything. She knew what was going on, and I think she was trying to be supportive but also give me the space I needed.

oooooooooo

"I hope you're planning on coming back," Wes called as we reached the door.

I hadn't participated in any more demonstrations, and at the moment was only thinking about getting home and taking a hot bath.

"Maybe," I sighed as I shook my head. I could feel the tears gathering at the back of my eyes, but I was determined not to let them fall. Richard had had enough of my tears, and I also knew once I started I'd have a hard time making them stop. I was tired of being seen as weak. I needed to get past this, and I finally was getting a support system in place.

As much as it helped going out with friends the night before, this right here is what I really needed.

"I'll meet you at the car," Erin murmured when her eyes made contact with someone behind me.

My face paled as I went back into high alert mode, and shook my head vigorously from side-to-side.

"Easy," he uttered behind me. "I'm not the enemy here." I turned, and saw the pleading eyes of Cole staring back at me. "I'm sorry," he shook his head slowly. "Whatever you went through that got you to this place," he waved his arms around "it's really fucked you up. No one should be this upset at a self-defense class."

I swallowed the lump in my throat and cast my eyes downward, "It's ok. It's not you. I swear it's not you."

He nodded silently before tipping my chin up to make eye contact with him, "I hope you'll come back. Whatever it is you're fighting I hope you'll come back and let me help you."

"Maybe," I murmured as I shifted on my feet. "I don't know if I can fight it. I might be broken beyond repair," I shrugged my shoulders as I stepped back away from him and shuffled out the door.

I knew it was a mistake coming here. I knew as soon as Erin told me what we were doing, that I'd end up a mess before we left. I should have insisted that she take me back home. Now I was stuck. Stuck in a situation that I should never have been in in the first place. I knew I'd go back. I knew the minute I looked into his dark, pleading eyes that I'd never be able to tell him no. He had me right where he wanted me. I didn't know how it would happen, but Cole Walker was going to turn my world on its axis.

ooooooooo

Cole

What the hell is going on here? When I wrapped my arms around Maddie for the demonstration, she sagged against me. It was like she wasn't even gonna fight. I watched Wes's face go from confused to panic. He'd seen this before. This woman wasn't here to prevent something bad from happening. She was here to learn how to keep it from happening again.

I could feel her heart hammering against my arm where I had it wrapped across her chest. Her breathing was coming in short bursts, and the trembling started soon after. Holy shit...this woman was going to have a panic attack right here in my arms.

I loosened my hold as I watched Wes give a slight nod. It was a cue we'd worked out for when a demonstration didn't go as planned. He quickly moved on to another person in the class while I worked to get Maddie back to her seat.

"Are you ok?" I murmured next to her ear.

"No...no I'm not," she shook her head.

I placed my hands on her shoulders, and began guiding her back to her seat. She sank down onto the chair as her face went completely blank of any expression. I don't know what happened to her, but someone really did a number on her. She went from smiling and happy, to completely shut down in a matter of seconds.

As the class continued, she sat there zoned out. Her friend spoke hushed words to her, but they elicited very little reaction from her.

When the class was over, I watched as she and her friend made their way to the door to leave. Her friend, Erin I think her name was, smiled at me and gave a slow nod. She got the silent message that I wanted to speak to Maddie alone. She murmured something in Maddie's ear and then made her way towards the door to the parking lot.

"Easy," I reached out to touch her shoulder. "I'm not the enemy here." I turned her to face me only she dropped her eyes to stare at the floor. "I'm sorry," I shook my head slowly. "Whatever you went through that got you to this place," I waved my arms around "it's really fucked you up. No one should be this upset at a self-defense class."

She swallowed as she continued to stare at the floor, "It's ok. It's not you. I swear it's not you." Her whispered plea was so quiet that I could barely hear the begging in it.

I nodded before using my index finger to tip her chin up to make eye contact with me, "I hope you'll come back. Whatever it is you're fighting…I hope you'll come back and let me help you."

"Maybe," she murmured as she shifted on her feet. "I don't know if I can fight it. I might be broken beyond repair," she shrugged her shoulders and looked away as she stepped back away from me and shuffled out the door.

I don't know what it was about her, but she made me feel something. My broken soul was calling to her. It sensed that whatever she was fighting, I was fighting too. We didn't know it yet, but we were more alike than we ever imagined. I just hoped that I wouldn't break her further.

Chapter 8

Maddie

"I am determined to have a good week," I stated as firmly as I could while I dressed for work. It was Monday again, and I was hoping for a fresh start. I hadn't had any nightmares last night, and I took that as a sign that the week was going to be great.

Erin and I had gone to a meeting, and then grabbed a coffee last night. We'd talked for a while about going back to McKay's. She was determined to get me there, but I just don't think I'm ready for that step yet. I know it's been five years, but they've been rough. I've actually come a long way in that time. When I first got away from Richard, I was afraid to leave the house. Now, I was working and hanging out with friends. Someone on the outside might even think I was almost normal.

I finished tying my sneakers, grabbed my ID badge, and made my way out to my car. It was a crisp spring morning, and I was hoping to make it to the dog park before my first patient.

oooooooooo

When I arrived at the office, Hannah was already unlocking the place and setting up for the day. Jo was going over the appointment book, and Ben and Jenny were setting up the exam rooms.

"Morning!" I called as I breezed in the door.

"Good morning," Hannah smiled brightly at me. "Heading out with Zeb?"

"Yeah," I nodded as I hooked my jacket over a peg by the door. "I haven't been able to get out much the last few days. I feel bad for him."

"Well, have fun," she grinned. "You don't have anyone coming in for another hour."

"Thanks, see ya," I waved as I headed back to the boarding room.

Zeb must have heard me coming because when I rounded the corner he was pawing at the door to his crate and whining.

"Hey Buddy," I called as I grabbed a leash. "Wanna go play?"

He whined again and then waited for me to unlock the door. After letting him out, I waited a minute as he bounced around. Once he calmed, I clicked the leash to his collar, and began leading him to the door. "I'll be back in an hour," I called over my shoulder as I shoved the door open, and let him lead me outside.

ooooooooo

Cole

I hate Mondays. I don't know what it is about them, but they never turn out the way I want them to. My alarm didn't go off when I set it, so now I was running late to work. Wes and I had discussed adding another time slot to our classes, and Monday morning was going to be it. I didn't really agree with that. I had wanted to spend it sleeping off the hangover I had from being out the night before. Plus there was Maddie. Sweet Maddie. I don't know where that came from, but she was in my head, and I couldn't get her out. I had tried, oh man I had tried.

~ 86 ~

I'd gone to Vibe last night hoping to find a hot little number to bring home and bury myself in, but nothing peaked my interest. It was like I was ruined, and I didn't even know this woman. Everyone I saw I found myself comparing them to her. They didn't have the right hair, or the right smile, or a tight little body.

She was perfect, and I know this from the little bit of time that I held her in my arms. The way she fit against my chest. Her soft curves against my hard angles. It would bring any man to his knees.

Seeing her on Friday night, and then at the gym on Saturday had been such a rush. It was the universe was trying to tell me something. I wasn't sure what, but I knew that Maddie held the key. Would I ever be able to help her though? Would she even let me try?

I'd had a fucked up childhood to say the least. Wes and I had been buddies since the third grade, and he knew my dad. He knew what my dad had done to my mom, sister, and me. Between the three of us, I think Mom got it the worst, but I got my fair share…that was certain. I'd buried the memories so far down that I wasn't sure they even existed anymore until Maddie had had her meltdown. When I felt her tremble in my arms, it all came back. All the nights of trying to protect my mom from *his* drunken rage. All the mornings of helping my sister get ready for school because Mom was so broken she couldn't get out of bed.

My childhood had been anything but happy. My father had slowly sucked every ounce of sunshine out of it. He'd systematically broken each of us painfully slow. My mom had never had the strength to stand up to him. My sister was too afraid to fight back, but me. I hated the bastard, and everything he did to us. When I'd met Wes, he'd offered me an escape. He'd let me stay with him when I'd suffered a beating, so I could rest without the worry of another attack. It didn't help as much as it should have though because when I wasn't at home I constantly worried about my mom. Was she taking the beating that was meant for me?

As I grew in size, so did my desire for revenge. The mean streak that my father had had begun to grow in me the way it did in him. I buried it, ashamed of what I was becoming. I'd never hit a woman before, but as anger and resentment began to grow in me, I slowly began to fear that I would one day. My father had done nothing to teach me the right way to care for someone. He'd shown me that when you didn't get what you wanted, you just hit the person and yelled at them until they gave in. He constantly reminded my sister that she was never planned. He told her daily that her whore of a mother made a choice that he didn't agree with. I watched my sister fight her demons for years before she met Caleb and found her self-worth.

Now as I run all the different scenarios through my head on why Maddie is the way she is, I can't help but worry that I'll get too close. She could never love me after what I did all those years ago.

I've only snapped once. One time. One time in my entire life and it changed the way I viewed the world forever. My mom didn't forgive me, and my sister didn't at first. Now that she's gotten away, I think she understands me better, but Maddie? What would Maddie think if she knew what I was capable of? Would she even talk to me? Would she give me a chance? Would she let me help her? I've been running those questions through my head all morning.

Now, as I stand here in Cool Beans waiting for my order, I can't help but think that Maddie would run screaming in the other direction if she knew what I did all those years ago.

oooooooooo

Maddie

When we reached the dog park, I went through my morning routine of letting Zeb take off. It took very little for him to realize he was free, and bolt. There wasn't a large crowd this early…that's one of the things I liked about coming in the morning.

I scanned the area, something that had become a habit, before making my way over to a bench. I chose a spot where I could see Zeb playing, and lowered myself onto it. As I sat there, thoughts of Cole flitted through my mind. I wondered where he was, what he was doing, and if I'd see him today. He'd said that this was where he'd first seen me. I don't know why I was concerned. I shouldn't have been. There was something about him though. It was like he understood me. I didn't think that was even possible though. Most men see a beautiful woman. They want to get to know her, but as soon as they find the baggage, they bolt. I didn't just have baggage, and I had a friggin' freighter.

"Hey," came a soft voice beside me. I hadn't even heard him approach, and jumped when he spoke.

"Uh hi?" I glanced up to see Cole staring down at me.

"Can I sit with you today? You're not going to run away again are you?" his lips curved up on one side as his eyes softened.

"Sure," I swallowed as I slid down the bench to make room for him.

"Coffee?" he held his hand out and in it was a paper cup with the Cool Beans logo on the front. "I wasn't sure how you took it, but this has cream and sugar."

"That's perfect. Thanks," I murmured as I brought the cup to my lips and took a tentative sip. We had sat there in silence for a few moments before he began talking again.

"I know you don't know me, but I'd like to get to know you better," he shifted, so he was angled more in my direction. "I wanna help."

"Help?" I looked away. "No one can help me," I muttered dejectedly.

"That's not true," he shook his head and released a sigh. "I think..." he scrubbed his palm down his face, "I think that you just need someone to help you fight back."

"Huh?" I turned to face him only to be met by the most startling chocolate eyes I'd ever seen. They had tiny gold flecks in them that sparkled with a hint of sadness.

"Let me help you take back some control," he tentatively reached out and placed his hand over mine where it was resting on my thigh. My eyes went wide, and I felt my muscles tighten.

"Sorry," he murmured. "You don't like being touched, do you?"

"No," I mumbled. "I don't like what I associate touching with."

"Come back to the gym with me," he begged. "Just you and me…any time you want. I'll teach you how to be the way you used to be."

"You don't even know the old me. She's been lost for so long, I don't think she can be found."

"I'll help you find her," his eyes pleaded as he looked away out over the rolling hills of the park. "I know you can find her. I understand more than you think."

I furrowed my brow as he continued to avoid making eye contact. How could any man know what it was like to be berated and beaten on a daily basis? Weren't men the strong ones? Weren't they supposed to be the protectors?

"Trust me," he sighed and his shoulders slumped. "I get it," he turned to stare into my eyes "more than you think."

We sat there in silence staring out at nothing in particular just enjoying each other's company. It was an odd feeling that he created in me. One I wasn't used to. The warning flares that had fired at the first several encounters we'd had seemed to have disappeared, and were now replaced with a sense of understanding. The pain I'd seen the other day at the gym had shown me a little bit of the man beneath the tough exterior. He may have been gorgeous and built like a brick wall, but underneath it all…I had a feeling was a scared little boy.

"I have to head into work," he murmured as he stood and tossed his coffee cup in a nearby trash can. "Think about what I said. I'm at McKay's every day. We can get the real you back, but you have to trust me."

"I'll think about it," I slowly nodded as I turned too and glanced back to where Zeb was rolling in the grass.

"See ya around Maddie," he called in a sad voice as he turned and walked away.

A sharp pang squeezed my chest as I turned and watched his retreating form. His broad shoulders were slumped in defeat as his feet kicked at the rocks while he walked away. I don't know what caused me to do it, but I soon found myself standing and calling out to him.

"Hey Cole?" I shouted.

He turned, and waited for me to continue, "Yeah?"

"Does tomorrow work?" I chewed the inside of my mouth. "To get the real me back? Will tomorrow work?"

"Sure," he smiled at me. "Come by whenever you want. I'll be there all day."

"Thanks," I called back as I turned to grab Zeb's leash. My time was up at the dog park, and I needed to get back to work myself.

"No problem," he grinned. "See ya tomorrow," he turned with an obvious pep in his step and left.

What had I done? I asked myself this a thousand times throughout the day. I was taking my life back, and that's what, and Cole Walker was going to help me. I don't know why, but the conversation we'd had in the park was just the push that I'd needed to do this. I would get the old me back no matter what it took.

Chapter 9

Maddie

"So you're really going to do it huh?" Erin nudged me and grinned as we walked out of St. Matthew's together.

"I'm gonna try," I shrugged as I fumbled with my keys. "I need to change something, and he wants to help, so…it seemed like a good idea."

"A good idea?" she giggled as we walked through the parking lot heading towards our cars. "It's a great idea! He's hot, and he's offering to let you beat up on him. I wish Wes would offer me lessons," she slowly shook her head like she was trying to clear it.

"Wait!" I stumbled slightly as I pulled us to a stop. "Do you have a thing for him?"

"No...yes...maybe? I don't know," Erin sighed. "I don't know if he's just being nice, or if he's interested. I think he's interested, but then he acts the same way he does with me, with everybody. I suck at reading people...at least with men, I do."

"You're putting too much pressure on yourself. He's a nice guy. Give it time, I guess. I mean...what do I know," I rolled my eyes and blew out a deep breath.

"So when are you planning to go back?" she grinned at me and wagged her brows.

"Tomorrow night after work," we had reached my car and I was in the process of tugging the door open.

"Well...." She paused and leaned in close like she was trying to share a secret, "Text me when you're finished. I want to know how it goes."

"What exactly do you think is going to happen?" I swallowed as embarrassment washed over me.

"I think you're going to the gym where a very delicious man is going to be wrapping his arms around you, and you get to rub against him without worrying about it going anywhere. You'll be able to think about that at night when you're all alone. I think you should use this time to test your limits," she tossed her arms in the air as if I was asking some of the dumbest questions on the planet.

"Maybe I shouldn't go," I muttered.

"What? No! You should definitely go," she narrowed her eyes at me. "Go, and tell me everything," she winked before heading over to her car and climbing in. "Don't leave out any details, and don't you dare back out!"

"Yeah...ok," I groaned as I climbed in my own car to go home. I knew I'd spend the evening trying to talk myself into doing this tomorrow. As much as I'd convinced myself that it was no big deal, and I could trust Cole, there was still that nagging feeling in the pit of my stomach that said otherwise.

oooooooooo

Cole

"She's not gonna show. I just know she's not," I shook my head woefully as I leaned against the front counter. I'd been parked here for the last hour waiting on Maddie. We closed at seven on Tuesday nights, and it was already six-thirty.

"Give her a chance bro," Wes mumbled from behind the counter. "I'm sure coming, here again, after what happened last weekend is gonna be hard. This place doesn't bring her good memories."

"I thought I'd made some progress at the park yesterday though. She seemed almost open to the idea," I turned so I could now face the door. "Dude, you gotta tell me what you know about her."

"Huh?" Wes's head snapped up. "I don't know anything about her.

"But you said to be careful..." I trailed off as I narrowed my eyes at him.

"Her friend is a member at one of the groups that I did a demo for. I just assumed," he shrugged without finishing. "After what happened Saturday, I think I assumed right."

"Oh something happened to her, I just wish she'd talk to me," I grumbled as I picked up at stack of papers on the counter and straightened them for the tenth time.

"Would you stop?" Wes smacked my hand. "You're going to drive yourself nuts. If she said she'd be here, then give her a chance to show. Stop being such a girl," he grinned at me.

"It's just something about her. I can't put my finger on it, but I just want to be around her. It's like she's this delicate broken thing, and I want to fix her."

"Well," his eyes rose towards the door, and he nodded slightly with his chin, "I think you're gonna get your chance."

I felt it almost instantly. She was here. I hadn't turned around, but the air in the room got thicker. My skin began to tingle slightly, and every nerve ending in my body went on high alert. I slowly turned around to glance in the direction Wes had nodded, and sure enough…there she was. Her lips curved up on one side slightly as she stood shifting her weight from foot to foot. A black gym bag hung over one shoulder, and water bottle was clutched tightly in her hand.

I jogged over to her and smiled, "You made it!"

She nodded before casting her eyes downward, and wrapping her arms around her middle in a defensive pose. I'd seen this with my sister…she was scared of me still.

"Let's put your things back here," I motioned towards the back of the gym, "and then we can get started."

"Ok," she whispered as she began chewing on the inside of her cheek.

oooooooooo

Maddie

"You can sit your things here," Cole pointed to a bench along the wall in the far corner of the gym. "We'll work right over here," he pointed to some mats that were spread out in a large square.

"Is this not a busy night?" I glanced around at the dwindling crowd.

"We're closing in half an hour," Cole answered without turning to look at me as he made his way over to the mats.

"Oh, I'm sorry. Why didn't you tell me? I can come back another time. I don't want…" I was cut off as he spun on me.

"My best friend owns this place," he waved his arms around. "I can come and go anytime I want. You're here now…so we're gonna work," he smirked at me. "Besides," he shrugged, "Wes says I need a good ass kicking today anyway."

"And you think I can kick your ass?" I tipped my head down and stared at myself before directing my gaze back at him. "I'm like half your size."

"Size doesn't matter," he chuckled when I started blushing. "Well, in this case anyway," he began strapping pads on his body. "With the right moves even a little thing like yourself can bring someone my size to their knees."

"Really?" I began walking slowly out onto the mat.

"Yeah...now come here," he motioned for me to stand in front of him. "You're not gonna hurt me, so don't hold back...got it?"

"Ok, but what if I?" I started to argue with him, but he scowled, so I snapped my mouth shut instantly. I'd seen that look with Richard, and I didn't want to start an argument with the one man who was trying to help me.

"You won't hurt me," he narrowed his gaze.

"Got it," I nodded as I grabbed the hem of my sweatshirt and ripped it over my head.

I saw Cole falter for a moment as he stood there taking me in. I'd dressed just like I did the first time I came...black stretch pants and a sports bra. I wasn't trying to impress anyone, but I guess he found me attractive...I wasn't real sure. It had been so long that I sometimes missed the signs.

Once I moved in front of him, he turned me to face away from him. "I'm gonna wrap my arms around you just like we did in class. If it gets to be too much, just tell me to stop, ok?"

I nodded as I felt him creep closer. Before I knew it, his arms wrapped around me like a steel band. He pressed himself into my back, but it felt more like he was cradling me than restraining me.

"Now, lift your arm like we talked about in class and bring your elbow back towards my nose," he spoke softly but firm, and I could feel his breath blowing over my cheek and neck.

I nodded again before shifting my weight and following his instructions. In one fell swoop I jerked and slammed my arm back. I felt it make contact with him, and his hold loosened enough that I was able to step away from him. Even though it wasn't much, and I had a long way to go, the idea that I'd done this sent a sense of pride rushing through me.

"I did it," I smiled as I spun to face him.

He nodded as he rubbed his cheek, "That you did." When he removed his hand, I noticed a red welt beginning to form.

"Oh no!" I gasped. "Did I hurt you?"

"Nah," he shook his head slightly. "This is nothing. Let's do it again, but this time I'm gonna make you work a little harder for it."

I swallowed, "Ok."

He spun me, so my back was to him once again, and wrapped his arms around me. This time, they tightened, and he lifted me slightly, so my feet weren't firmly planted. "Come on! Fight back!" he commanded as I started to struggle. "Teach me not to mess with you."

"No!" I shouted right before I slammed my elbow back once again this time making direct contact with his nose.

"Sonofa," he groaned when his arms released me.

I spun around to him cupping his nose as blood leaked between his fingers. "Oh my god! I'm so sorry! I didn't mean it," I began backing away toward my bag. Memories of the few times I'd inflicted pain on Richard surged to the forefront of my mind. What was he gonna do to me now? He shook his head as he squatted and pinched the bridge of his nose. When his eyes made contact with mine, I didn't see rage...instead I saw question.

oooooooooo

Cole

Sonofabitch that hurt! I knew better than to not duck out of the way, but when I've got her right there in my arms, I don't want to get out of the

~ 103 ~

way. I was so sidetracked when I put her in the hold again, that I didn't move when I saw her elbow coming right for my face.

Now here I am, slumped over, trying to get this fucker to stop bleeding, and she's cowering in the corner. The few times I looked at her, and she'd gone from proud of herself to afraid. I wanted to assure her that I was fine, but at the moment my head was a little fuzzy. I don't know if it was the blow to the head that I just took, or having Maddie so close.

"I'm ok," I lifted the hand that wasn't pinching my nose and waved it at Maddie. "This isn't something new." I watched her slowly inch away from me like she was preparing to bolt. "Oh no, you don't," I muttered to myself as I grabbed the hem of my t-shirt and yanked it off. I balled it in my hand and held it to my nose to stop the bleeding while I made my way over to where she was digging in her gym bag.

When I got to her, I squatted down behind her and slowly reached out to touch her shoulder. She flinched slightly before turning her head to glance back at me.

"I didn't mean to," she squeaked as her eyes went wide with fear.

"I know," I whispered as I slowly lowered my now bloody shirt. The bleeding had finally stopped, and I wanted to try and convince her to stay. "I'm fine...see?"

She sucked her lip in and clamped her teeth down as she nodded slowly. "Really...I didn't," she glanced away and inhaled a shaky breath.

"I'm not mad at you," I tried again. "It was my fault really. I didn't get out of the way."

"Why?" she mumbled without looking me in the eyes.

I placed my finger under her chin and tipped her head so I could make eye contact, "You're distracting."

"Me?" her eyes were sad and confused.

"You distract me when I'm around you. All I could think about was that fact that you were trusting me enough to touch you," I shrugged before tossing my shirt off to the side. She had continued to stare at it, and I wanted to show her I really was fine. "Wanna try the other moves you learned on Saturday? I promise I'll move this time," I grinned at her as I stood and held out my hand for her to take.

She nodded slightly as she reached out and took it. "Sure," she smiled as she stood and squared her shoulders.

I turned and began to pull her back out into the center of the mat, but she held fast to my hand

and didn't move. I turned to peer back at her and furrow my brow as she stood stock still staring at me, "You coming?" Her head slowly moved from side-to-side. "What's wrong?"

"What happened to you," the words came out strangled as she slapped her free hand over her mouth and her eyes went wider.

"What?" I couldn't figure out what she was talking about, and look on her face was beginning to worry me.

She pointed at my shoulders and asked again, "That...what happened?" Tears welled in her eyes like she already knew the answer but was afraid to hear it from me.

I had completely forgotten about the scars when I had whipped my shirt off. I was so used to people ignoring them that I didn't even think she would notice, but then again...we were more alike than she knew.

"I told you I understood more than you know," I cocked my head to the side. "Now...are you coming?"

She gave a slow nod before moving closer to me, "Do you want to talk about it?" she asked sadly.

"No, not right now. Right now I want to teach you how to kick my ass. My past is not something that you need floating around in your head right now. Trust me," I shook my head slowly.

"Ok," she agreed like she understood that I was unwilling to talk about it, but I could tell by the questioning look in her eyes that she was going to bring the topic up again sometime soon, and I had no idea how much I was willing to tell her.

Could I open up? Could I confide in a stranger things that I hadn't even told my best friend? Would she even want to be around me once she knew the truth about me? Probably not. I couldn't tell her. I had to keep my secret buried. No matter what…I couldn't tell her about my father.

Chapter 10

Cole

When she finally began to shuffle behind me, I breathed a sigh of relief. I'd gotten her to drop the topic. I knew by the look on her face that she'd bring it up again, but at the moment I just wanted to get her past whatever had flashed through her mind when she'd hit me.

"All right," I turned her, so her back was to me. "When I grab you again, I want you to use your right foot. Step back, and stomp as hard as you can. Got it?"

She nodded and tensed slightly, "You're gonna move, right? You're not going to let me hurt you, are you?"

I couldn't help but chuckle slightly, "I'll move. I promise."

She nodded again, and as soon as I tightened my arms around her, she shouted, "No!" and stepped back causing us both to trip and fall to the mats. I rolled to the side, but still kept my arms wrapped around her. She tensed when she felt me press into her back.

If I had any sense, I would have released her immediately, but she felt so good pressed against me that I just wanted it to last a little longer. I reached up and ran my palm along her arm lightly. "Relax," I murmured as I watched her face get whiter and whiter. "You're ok."

"Please let go of me," she whispered in a frightened tone.

I sighed and released my hands from where they gripped her body. Watching the realization that she was free wash over her face was like watching her melt. She'd gone from stiff and ashen, to pliable in a matter of seconds. The relief that filled her shaking body was somewhat disconcerting to me. What had I done that upset her so much other that touch her? What had happened to her that she was so afraid of anyone being anywhere near her?

"You wanna try something else?" I smiled as I pushed myself to my feet and offered her a hand to stand.

She glanced around the now empty gym before looking back at me, "Are you guys closed?"

I scanned the room until my eyes met the clock hanging on the front wall, "Yeah...but like I said. We can stay as late as we want. Wes won't care."

"Um...I really should get home," she was shuffling her feet at this point and looking at everything but me.

"I'll make sure you get home all right," I lifted a shoulder. I really wanted her to stay. I still hadn't figured her out, and with us being here alone I was hoping that she would open up a little more for me.

"Well..." she twisted her fingers together. "I guess I can stay a little longer. What's next?"

"How about we have some fun?" I wiggled my brows.

"Fun?" she swallowed. "What kinda fun?"

"Wanna learn how to punch?" I began walking over to a box that held all sorts of equipment. I leaned over and began digging through it looking for some boxing gloves that would fit my little fairy.

"Like fight?" her eyes flashed with a nervousness that I thought we'd gotten past.

"Sure," I shrugged before I held up a pair of gloves.

Her head slowly began to shake as she began backing up towards where her bag was tossed on the floor. "I don't think that's a good idea," she murmured.

"Why not?" I cocked my head to the side. "I know someone hurt you. I know you're keeping it hidden from the world. You think no one gets you, and no one cares," I continued to advance towards her as she slowly backed away. "I've been there. I might not know your story," I tossed my head back and blew out a breath, "but I know you need to let it out." I had finally reached her at this point, and I handed her the gloves. "Put these on, and wale on me. Take out whatever you're holding back, and release it. You'll feel so much better when do, and maybe then you can finally trust me. I promise…I'm not gonna get mad, or hurt you."

She looked up at me with a sadness that I recognized and sucked her lip into her mouth, "That's what they all say."

It was so quiet that I'd almost missed it. "All?" I crept closer.

She nodded as a tear slipped down her cheek, "Bet you didn't think I was this damaged huh?"

"You're not damaged. You just have a past...we all do. I'm trying to help you stand up against it. Now," I handed her the boxing gloves and pushed her towards the mat. "Put those on, and I'll help you tighten them."

Once I had her all set, I grabbed the pads for my arms and made my way over to stand in front of her.

"What do I do," she raised her hands out to the side before letting them drop again.

"Well," I smirked at her. "There's a correct form for all this, but tonight I want you to get all the aggression out. So... hit me!"

"What?" she gasped as her mouth dropped open in shock.

"Hit me!" I growled as held up a pad for protection. "As hard as you can...hit me!"

She pulled back her right arm, and then brought it across her body in a right cross, but when it hit the pads it was a little more than a gentle flick. She shook her head and sighed to herself.

"I'm sorry...that was lame."

"Not lame...but put your weight behind it," I nodded. "Again!"

"Ahhh!" she screamed as she pulled back and swung again. This time when her fist connected with the pad I had to brace myself.

"Better...again!" I nodded and prepared for the assault. Once she was ready, she rocked back and swung her entire body into it. As soon as her right fist made contact, she swung the left. In a quick succession, she managed to land a good ten punches before stopping to take a break.

"Where did that come from?" I smiled at her as she hunched over and placed her fists on her knees. She was breathing hard, and her hair had slipped out of her ponytail and was sticking to her sweaty face.

"I don't know," she panted as she tried to catch her breath. "It felt good though," she tipped her face up to stare at me and a grin broke out across it.

"Wanna go again?" I teased.

"Can we?" her excitement was contagious as she stood and wiped her hair off her brow.

"Sure…I can go all night," I smirked at her. I liked this side of Maddie. It was fun and playful, and I'd never seen it before. When she was like this, I was willing to do just about anything.

We spent the next hour going back and forth between punching and kicking. I'd gotten her to get her feet involved, and now she was giving me quite a workout.

"That was amazing," I grinned at her as I watched her pace back-and-forth on the mats. "There's more in you than you thought huh?"

"I can't believe I just did all that," she gasped for air as she began loosening the gloves and tossing them to the ground. "I need some water," she panted as she began to walk towards her bag and grab a water bottle.

Once she reached it, and she threw her head back and gulped the water down before letting a small amount run over her face. I stood there just watching her. She was amazing, and nothing like what I ever expected. I knew I needed her in my life, and I just wasn't sure how to go about it. Having her here at the gym was great, but I wanted more.

"Wanna go another round," I asked from directly behind her. I'd moved to get closer, but

I don't think she'd heard me. She jumped almost instantly when I'd started talking.

"I really should be getting home. I've got to work early tomorrow," she dropped the water bottle onto of her bag.

I placed my hand on her shoulder, and she stiffened slightly. "I'd really like to spend some more time with you," I murmured.

"Here?" she squeaked.

"Here, or dinner maybe?" I let my hands trail lightly down her arms and watched as goose bump rose in their wake.

"I don't know…" she shook her head as her voice changed from the happy, confident woman that had stood before me mere moments ago into the sad scared one I'd met in the park.

"Please Maddie? I want a chance…that's all I'm asking. A chance to show you we're not all bad," I stepped back as she started to turn.

"How do you know about *him*?" she narrowed her eyes at me. "How do you know it was a man? You don't know anything about me!" anger spread through her features as she spat the words at me.

"I don't," shook my head and sighed. "I don't know who did this to you, but I do know you're afraid of me. I know whatever happened to you was at the hands of a man. I know he broke your trust. I know you think that we're all like him. I know that it's going to be an uphill battle for me or any other man in your life..." I let the silence build between us as I dropped my gaze from hers.

She stood there for the longest time just chewing on her lip and fidgeting with a loose piece of hair. "I'm sorry," she muttered. "Thank you for this, but I don't think I can give you more yet. I'm sorry," she continued to mumble as she backed away from me, grabbed her gym bag, and scurried for the door.

"I'm here every day," I shouted at her back. "Come by anytime, and I'll help you!"

"Thanks!" she called over her shoulder as she pushed through the door, and out into the night.

ooooooooo

Maddie

What just happened? As I climbed into my car, I glanced back at the door to McKay's. My heart was racing, and my hands were still trembling. *Did he just ask me out? He did, and I turned him down. I cranked the car and began pulling out of the parking lot to head for home.*

Why did I turn him down? He's so hot, and he seems like a nice guy.

I couldn't stop my inner monologue the entire way home. Cole had put me on edge, and at the moment I couldn't remember why I told him no. Maybe it was that feeling that he caused in me. That had to be it. He made my insides come alive, and feel things that had been absent in my life for years. That tingling that you get when you're near someone? That heat that surges through your system telling you that your body wants whatever it's near? Cole brought that out in me. Whenever he was nearby, my body seemed to call to him. It wanted to be wrapped in his arms, and as much as that idea scared me it also turned me on.

I cursed myself as I pulled into my parking spot and yanked my car door open. I couldn't be with him no matter what my traitorous body wanted. He was a man. He was dangerous. He'd never want me if he knew the whole story, he just thought he did.

I grabbed my gym bag out of the back seat as I made my way into my apartment building and headed for the elevators. I needed a cool shower to rid myself of thoughts of Cole. I needed to wash them away just like the salty sweat that now coated my body.

oOoooooOo

After stripping out of my clothes, I stepped into the spray and sighed in relief. The cool water felt heavenly, and I knew I'd be sore in the morning from the punishing workout I'd given myself. True, it felt good to release all the tension I'd had built up the last several days, but I wasn't used to working out like that...ever.

I don't know what it was about Cole, but my initial feelings about him had changed. The danger that I'd felt at that first meeting at the park had morphed into understanding. I let the water run over my face, and I closed my eyes. Pictures of Cole flashed through my mind as I stood there letting the evening wash away. I silently wondered what his story was. Why did he want to help so badly? What had happened to him that he felt the need to protect me? Essentially, that's what he was doing. He was giving me the courage to fight back...to take back my life...but why?

Visions of his scarred back floated through my mind, and my eyes flashed open. Who had done that to him, and why? What had he ever done to deserve that? Surely it wasn't something that he had allowed. He had said that he understood me...did he really?

My head was spinning, and the more I thought about it, the worse I felt. Should I have said yes when he asked me out? No, I'm glad I didn't. I wasn't ready for something like that, but... there was still something about him that made me want to know more.

I turned the water off and stepped out of the shower still shaking my head at my thoughts. I needed to go back. Back to the gym, and back to Cole. I needed to go back and see where this went. If anything...he could help me build my confidence up and finally take control of my life.

As I dressed myself in a pair of sleep shorts and a tank, I climbed into bed yawning as I flicked off the light. Tomorrow I would go back. I'd let him teach me how to fight back. I needed this, and by the sad look that Cole had had on his face tonight...he needed it too.

Chapter 11

Cole

After Maddie had raced out of the gym last night, I'd spent an extra hour on the speed bag. Now, I was regretting it as I stood in the boxing ring with my best friend while he kicked my ass.

"What's with you today?" Wes shook his head at me as he dropped his hands to his side.

"Nothing!" I growled as I grabbed my mouth guard and slipped it in my mouth. "Let's go!"

He sighed and lifted his hands in front of his body to block my punches. As soon as he was ready, I pulled my fist back and swung. He rocked back slightly and grinned at me. "Come on pretty boy. That all you got?"

"Shut up!" I grunted as I swung again.

"You suck today," he shook me off and tossed the pads to the side.

"What's that supposed to mean?" I rolled my eyes as I watched him.

"It means I'm done playing the punching bag. I'm gonna start hitting back," he smirked at me as he grabbed a pair of his own gloves. "You're going down Walker."

"Well see," I popped my neck and cracked my wrists as I watched him circle me.

I knew it was coming when he rounded on me, but my slow ass was tired tonight. So when Wes's fist connected with my jaw, I stumbled back slightly. I shook off the blow as I narrowed my eyes at him, "Fucker."

"Come on!" he taunted. "Show me what you got."

"You're a dead man!" I growled as I advanced towards him.

While my right hand swung at his face, my left went for his ribs. He stepped back to try and keep his balance, but I swept my foot under him causing him to fall back. When his rear hit the mat, he glared up at me.

"This isn't MMA fucker," he spit his guard out as I grinned down out at him. "What the hell?"

"Shut up you pussy and fight like a man," I turned my back on him and began to make my way over to where I'd left my water bottle.

I wasn't really paying attention to what he was saying, but I could hear him shouting something behind me. When I stood and tossed my water back to the ground, my eyes connected with the last person I expected to see. Maddie. She was standing about twenty feet from the ring and staring at me wide-eyed. I winked at her, and turned ready to resume the ass beating that I'd been handing out. Wes must have seen that I was distracted because he took full advantage. As soon as I started to turn, his fist connected with the side of my head.

I rocked to the side slightly in a daze. I'd been completely unprepared for the blow, and seeing the shock on Maddie's face sent me over the edge. I rounded on him and growled, "What the fuck was that for?"

Wes thought I was joking, and lifted his arms out to the side as he smirked at me. I stormed up and pushed against his chest. Anger causing my entire body to vibrate. "You're an asshole," I leaned in close and shoved him. The smile he'd been wearing dropped from his face, and he sobered quickly.

"Dude, I'm sorry. I thought you were ready," he glanced behind me, I'm assuming to see what had gotten me so worked up.

"You do that again, and I'll kick your ass for real," I growled.

Wes tipped his chin up and darted his eyes between me and somewhere behind me before slowly shaking his head. When I turned around, I saw Maddie had turned a pale white and was slowly backing away from where she'd been standing.

"Wait Maddie!" I held my hand up and began stripping my gear off as fast I could. "It's not what you think…" I trailed off as I climbed through the side of the ring and chased after her.

She was walking as fast as she could towards the door, and I knew if I didn't stop her, I might never see her again. "Wait," I called again as I reached out and clamped my hand down on her shoulder.

She spun around so fast, and I had to take a step back. "I can't do this," she shook her head frantically at me. "I promised myself I wouldn't do this again."

"Do what?" I gripped the back of my neck and scowled.

"This," she waved her arms in front of her.

"Wait, you mean that?" I pointed to the area I'd just come from. "What do you think was going on there?"

She shook her head slowly as she let her chin drop to her chest, "I don't know, but I do know that the look on your face said it all."

"What?" I stepped closer, so we were only a few inches apart. She swallowed before allowing her gaze to turn up to my face. "That was nothing," I pointed to where Wes was putting away the gear. "We're friends...that's how we blow off steam."

She glanced at Wes and then back at me before her gaze returned to him, "Blow off steam?"

"Yeah...like we were doing last night?" I shrugged as I waited to see what she would do next.

"Ok," she mumbled.

"Ok?" I stared at her as I watched her body relax slightly. "So...what's up?"

"I wanted to come back," she chewed her lip nervously. "I...I want to practice what we did last night."

"Sure," I couldn't help the grin that spread across my face. "Just don't be too hard on me," I chuckled. "Wes did a number on my jaw already."

"Doesn't look too bad," she smiled slightly.

"Well, I can't lose my good looks. How would I attract the ladies?" I smirked as I began walking to the back corner where we'd worked the night before.

"I think you look just fine," the words slipped out of her lips so quietly that I almost missed them.

I turned to look over my shoulder, and came face-to-face with a bright red Maddie. She was embarrassed, and she looked so cute.

"You do huh?" I stepped back a little and nudged her with my elbow.

"Na," she shook her head as the blush began to creep down her neck.

"It's ok you know," I winked at her, "that you think I'm hot."

She shook her head again as she stumbled slightly.

"Go out with me," I leaned in close to her ear and watched her body quiver.

"No," she tossed her bag to the floor. "I can't."

"You will...you'll see," I lifted a shoulder and turned to make my way out onto the mat. She'd give in eventually. I just needed to get her to trust me.

oooooooooo

Maddie

After spending the day convincing myself that I should go back, I was now standing in the parking lot of McKay's staring up at the sky. I knew this was a good thing...coming back here. If anything, I was learning how to defend myself, and Cole seemed genuinely to care. I took one last deep breath before I forced myself to walk through the doors. The sight I was met with shocked the hell out of me.

The tender caring man that had helped me the night before had morphed into something I was all too familiar with. He was drenched in sweat, and breathing heavily as he stalked around the boxing ring in the middle of the gym. He was shaking his head and muttering something as he made his way over to the corner. He leaned down and grabbed a water bottle before spitting out his mouth guard. Sweat was trickling down his body, and I couldn't help but stare as I watched his Adam's apple bob up and down as he swallowed. My heart rate picked up, and my ears began to buzz as I watched the next several seconds unfold in front of me.

The other guy in the ring came bustling up behind him, and taunted him just as he made eye contact with me. Cole grinned, and I couldn't help but smile back. Then as if in slow motion, I watched the other guy's fist rear back and come crashing into the side of Cole's head.

He rocked on his feet slightly and stumbled before turning toward the other guy. He yelled something, but I couldn't make it out. I was so shocked at what was happening that all I wanted to do was get away from them. Watching them go at it made me think of Richard, and I had no intention of being around anyone who was anything close to what Richard was.

I turned and began walking towards the door as fast as I could. I'd almost escaped the place when I felt a hand clamp down on my shoulder halting me, "Wait!" His panicked voice caused me to stiffen as I slowly turned to face him.

"I can't do this. I promised myself I wouldn't do this again," I was babbling but at the moment I just wanted to get out of there.

"Do what?" he gripped the back of his neck and scowled.

"This," I waved my arms around in front of me.

"Wait, you mean that?" he pointed to the area he'd just come from. "What do you think was going on there?"

I shook my head slowly as I let my chin drop to my chest, "I don't know, but I do know that the look on your face said it all."

"What?" he stepped closer, so we were only a few inches apart. I swallowed before allowing my gaze to turn up to his face. "That was nothing," he pointed to where the other guy was putting away the gear. "We're friends...that's how we blow off steam."

I glanced at his friend and then back at him before my gaze returned to his friend, "Blow off steam?"

"Yeah...like we were doing last night?" he shrugged.

"Ok," I mumbled trying to comprehend what had just happened.

"Ok?" he stared at me as I tried to relax. "So...what's up?"

"I wanted to come back," I chewed my lip nervously. "I...I want to practice what we did last night."

"Sure," he grinned at me. "Just don't be too hard on me," he chuckled. "Wes did a number on my jaw already."

"Doesn't look too bad," I smiled slightly.

"Well, I can't lose my good looks. How would I attract the ladies?" he smirked as he began walking to the back corner where we'd worked out the night before.

"I think you look just fine," the words slipped out of my mouth before I could stop them.

When he turned to look at me, I couldn't hide my embarrassment.

"You do huh?" he stepped back a little and nudged me with his elbow.

"Na," I shook my head as I tried to recover, but I could feel the blush begin to creep down my neck.

"It's ok you know," he winked at me, "that you think I'm hot."

I shook my head again and stumbled slightly. He knew…if he knew I thought he was attractive. I was so done for.

"Go out with me," he leaned in close to my ear.

"No," I tossed my bag to the floor. "I can't."

"You will…you'll see," he lifted a shoulder and turned to make his way out onto the mat as his grin spread to epic proportions.

ooooooooo

Over the next two weeks, I spent every afternoon at McKay's. Between work, going to meetings, and working out with Cole I had very little time to dwell on my past. Being busy helped in a way I didn't think possible. The dreams had almost disappeared completely, and I hoped with time I'd get my life back.

Cole had been relentless lately and asked me out at least once a day. Every time he would, I'd always respond with 'no', but he didn't seem to want to give up. I had hoped that he'd have stopped by now, but as I glanced down at the text message he'd sent me this morning I could see that it wasn't happening.

Cole: You coming by tonight?

Me: Yes, as soon as I leave work.

Cole: Go out with me Saturday?

I sighed as I read it over and over. I'd asked myself numerous times if I should give him a chance, but I always managed to talk myself out of it.

Pulling myself from my car, I grabbed my gym bag and made my way inside. I might as well get this over with.

"So did you think it over?" Cole smirked at me as I strapped the boxing gloves around my wrists.

"Think what over?" I played dumb, but I knew what he meant and by the look on his face, he knew that I knew.

"About Saturday," he rolled his eyes at me. We'd been playing this game on a daily basis, and as much as the idea of going on a date terrified me I was enjoying our banter.

"Can't," I shook my head as I made my way out onto the mat.

"Why's that?" he cocked his head to the side.

"I'm busy," I shrugged my shoulders as I stretched and got into position.

He sauntered over as he cracked his neck and put on a show. "How about if I beat you, you say yes?"

"No," I shook my head vehemently as he lifted his arm to prepare to block my fist.

"Fine," he huffed and grabbed my arm as it came at him.

We went back and forth for the next hour. Me throwing punches, and him defending himself against me. I knew that if he really wanted to, he could restrain me. He was bigger and heavier than me, but he'd taught me several escape holds and after I'd mastered them I'd demanded that he teach me how to fight back.

"You're getting so much better," he praised as he stepped back.

I was breathing hard, but I was pumped. As he moved back in position, I raced forward and put all my weight behind me as I swung my arm through the air. He surprised me this time by gripping my wrist and spinning me. He pressed his chest into my back as his arms banded around me. I tensed at first. I hadn't been comfortable in this position in a long time, but there was something about Cole that had begun to make it different. A month ago, I would have freaked out, but now it was almost soothing.

My chest heaved as I felt his heart thunder against my back. He dropped his chin down to my shoulder as he whisper, "You ok?"

I swallowed as I let my head bob up-and-down. My body trembled, and a shiver rippled through me. Why was I so turned on? What was it about Cole that did this to me?

"Shit," he muttered as he spun me to face him, and before I could react he leaned down and crashed his mouth into mine.

Chapter 12

Cole

Warm honey…that's the only way I could describe it. When I felt her tremble against me, it was all I could do to not pull us both to the ground and ravage her right there. Deciding that I'd take my chances with her reaction, I spun her in my arms and pressed my mouth to hers. She stiffened at first. It was almost like she wasn't sure what to do, but as I began to take control of the kiss she soon melted into me.

Her lips were soft and moved in a languid pace as her arms rose and wrapped around my shoulders. The boxing gloves prevented her from doing much, but by the way she clung to me I knew she was giving in. I let my tongue take a tentative swipe at her lower lip, and when she gasped I took full advantage. Slowly I began moving us toward the back corner of the gym. I didn't want to be on display for the other patrons, and I wasn't sure what Maddie would do when she came back to the present and realized what she'd done.

As soon as I took that first step, I felt her stumble so in true gentleman fashion I reached down to grab her thighs and lifted her into my arms. I almost couldn't believe it when I felt her legs wrap around me. Here was a woman who'd been turning me down for two weeks straight, and she was finally giving in.

oooooooooo

Maddie

What am I doing? Oh god, it feels so good, but what am I doing? When he kissed me, it happened so fast that I wasn't sure what I should do. Should I push him away? Should I pull back? Should I slap him? Within seconds of feeling his warm lips against mine, my body made the decision for me. *Give in…give in…give in…*it rang through my head like a mantra.

Cole took full advantage when I surrendered to him. I know he felt it the moment it happened. His arms wrapped around me as he crushed me to his chest. His hold was firm, but delicate at the same time...almost like he was afraid he'd break me. I felt his tongue take a swipe at my lower lip, and I gasped. When I moved my hands up to wrap around his shoulders, I groaned in frustration. The boxing gloves were still tied around my wrists, and were preventing me from running my fingers through his hair. I scrambled to get them off, and was completely taken off guard when I felt him lift me off the floor. Instinctively, I wrapped my legs around his waist as he started moving. I wasn't sure where he was taking me, but I was so turned on at the moment that I didn't care. I don't know what was happening to me. Why wasn't I afraid? Why wasn't I trying to stop this? What was wrong with me?

The boxing gloves fell to the floor as I felt my back press against the wall. Cole's hands stayed put right under my thighs holding me in place, but his mouth...that was another story. He trailed kisses over my jaw as he made his way to my ear. "What are you doing to me?" he panted. "Tell me to stop," he begged as he rolled his hips pressing his erection into my heated core.

"I don't know," I gasped as my now free hands slid into his hair and tugged lightly.

"Maddie?" he paused as he nipped my ear. "Go out with me."

I froze in place as a million different scenarios ran through my mind. Did I want that? Where was this going, and what would going on a date mean? Would he expect more now? Did he think going on a date meant sex? "I..." I shook my head as I leaned back and stared into his eyes. "I can't..." I released his hair where I'd been gripping it and pushed lightly on his shoulders.

He shook his head as he slowly stepped back and lowered me to the ground. As soon as my feet touched the ground, and I had my balance he stepped back completely.

"Did I read this wrong?" he shook his head at me. "Did you not feel anything right now?"

I could feel my face heating as I turned away from him, "I..."

"No," he shook his head again as he muttered to himself. "You wanted that as much as I did. I could feel it. Why won't you let me take you out on a date?"

"I just..." I stammered as I tried to turn away from him. I don't know why I was fighting this so much. I knew we had great chemistry, but the fear of letting someone into my life like that again had me pulling away faster than I could stop it.

"What did that fucker do to you?" he shook his head at me as confusion, pain of rejection, and sorrow filled his face. He moved closer as I stepped back. I felt my back hit the wall behind me once again as he moved so close we were almost touching. His eyes held an understanding as he tipped his chin down and blinked a few times. I could see something flit across his face, but it disappeared as fast as it showed up. "You deserve to be happy," he murmured as he lifted his hand to cup my cheek. I felt his thumb brush across the apple of my cheek as a sigh escaped his lips. "Please? Please let me show you." He squeezed his eyes shut before he leaned forward and brushed his lips across my forehead, "Please?"

"I…" I tried again to make the words come out, but my tongue felt heavy, and my brain was muddled. "Ok," I finally mumbled.

"Ok?" his head snapped up like he wasn't sure he'd heard me. "Is that a yes," his lips started to curve into a smile as he leaned closer.

I nodded as he touched his forehead to mine, "Yes, it's a yes."

"Great," he smirked. "Does Saturday work? Say seven?"

"Sure," I let my lips curve up on one side. "Saturday's fine."

"I'll pick you up then," his smile grew as he stepped back away from me.

"Pick me up?" my voice trembled and Cole's smile dropped immediately as he watched me.

"What's wrong?" he reached up to grab his neck.

"How do you know where I live?" my voice quivered as I started to tremble harder. How the hell was I going through so many emotions tonight was baffling to me.

"Um," he scratched his head. "It's on your registration form," his forehead wrinkled as he moved closer and placed his hand on my shoulder.

The shaking stopped as soon as he touched me, and I couldn't help but sigh in relief. It was as if his touch was a soothing balm, and as scared as I was to be anywhere near intimate contact, Cole's touch somehow helped.

"He really screwed up your sense of trust didn't he?" Cole murmured.

I couldn't do anything other than nod as I bit my lip, and glanced up at the sad chocolate eyes. "Yes," it slipped out as a whisper "But this helps."

"Good," he glanced back over his shoulder to peer around the gym before leaning down to grab my discarded gloves. "Let's finish this up. I think you might need to hit something right about now, and I'm afraid if we don't get back to it I might take advantage of you standing there against the wall."

As I watched him turn and step in the direction of the mat, I took a deep breath and swallowed. Was I ready for this? Could I go back to that place where happiness was optional? Could I give myself over to a man, and trust him to treat me, right? While I watched Cole get into position as he waited for me, I smiled to myself. With Cole, I thought anything might be possible. He seemed to understand me, in a way, that no one else had ever tried. He knew exactly when to push, and when to back off.

ooooooooo

Cole

As I made my way to Maddie's place, I couldn't help the nervous feeling that was sitting in the pit of my stomach. She had been so scared

~ 140 ~

when she realized that I knew where she lived. It was almost as if she was afraid to allow anyone any control over her in any situation. I knew that if I wanted her to trust me, I was going to need to let her set the pace of the evening.

I'd planned to take her to dinner, and maybe a movie after if she was feeling up to it. I was hoping she would. After yesterday's kiss at the gym, I had been counting the minutes until I could get her to snuggle up to me in a dark theater. The idea of her soft curves pressed against my side had been keeping me in a perpetual state of arousal all day.

When I finally made my way to her building, I parked on the street and headed into the lobby area. After pressing the buzzer and letting her know I was there, I stepped to the side and waited.

oooooooooo

Maddie

"This is it," I mumbled to myself as I took one last glance in the mirror. Cole had called up a moment ago, and I'd told him I'd be right down, but now I wasn't so sure.

The skirt I'd paired with a loose cotton top had seemed like a good idea at the time, but now I was second guessing myself. The black fabric swayed around my thighs and fluttered in the breeze I created when I walked. The bright pink top clung to me in all the right places, and the deep V-neck hinted at just the right amount of cleavage. I'd left my hair down in soft waves and used just enough makeup to highlight my features. I'd always been told that I had beautiful eyes, but with as many black eyes as I'd had over the years with Richard, it had become a habit to try and distract people from noticing them.

I shifted in front of the mirror again as I contemplated changing. Finally deciding that I'd just take a chance, I grabbed my purse and scurried out the door.

The elevator ride was quick, and by the time I reached the ground level I was more nervous than I cared to admit. When the doors opened to reveal a gorgeous man standing with his back to me, I couldn't help but gasp. Cole was truly a guy's guy. His broad shoulders filled out his black button down perfectly. He'd rolled the sleeves up to just below his elbows and paired it with a pair of worn jeans. He must have heard me gasp because he turned and glanced over his shoulder, and our eyes connected immediately. I couldn't help my body's reaction as I let my eyes travel the length of him. We'd spent every day for the last two weeks together at the gym, but gym rat Cole had nothing on this version. The top few buttons of his shirt were open revealing a smattering of dark chest hair, and his hair was tousled just enough to look stylish. He winked at me causing me to blush and look away.

"It's ok to look," he smirked. "You look nice too."

"Uh…thanks," murmured as I glanced down at my feet. "You're sure this is ok?"

"Maddie, you look beautiful. Don't think anything otherwise, ok?" He moved closer and offered me his hand, "You ready?"

I nodded as I reached out and linked our fingers together all the while staring up at him. Even as an adult, I still had that nervous fluttering in my belly like a teenager going out with her crush for the first time.

He tugged me closer to his side as he leaned down and whispered in my ear, "Stop worrying. It's gonna be a good night."

"I trust you," I murmured as he led me out to his Explorer that was parked on the street in front of my building. And I did…trust him…I just wasn't sure if I trusted myself. I built these walls along time ago to prevent things like this from happening, and one-by-one Cole Walker was slowly tearing them down. What would he think of me when he finally stripped me bare of all my insecurities? Would he like the person he found? Would he still want me? Had Richard destroyed me to the point that there was nothing left? I had no idea what the answer to any of those question was, but I was silently hoping that I would soon find out.

Chapter 13

Cole

Once I had her seated in my car, I jogged around to the driver's side, climbed in, and pulled out into traffic. The restaurant I'd picked out was on the waterfront at the harbor, and as we headed in that direction, I couldn't help but watch the smile on Maddie's face grow.

"Are we going to the beach?" she turned to look at me and grin.

"Sort of," I lifted a shoulder as I let my arm drape across the steering wheel. "I found this place a few months ago, and if you like fish...it's the place to be."

"I love seafood," her smile grew as she shifted in the seat.

"I know," I winked at her.

"Wait," her face paled "how do you know that?"

"I asked Erin," I cocked my head to the side as I studied her. "She came by to talk to Wes last night, and I asked her where she thought I should take you." I couldn't figure out why she was suddenly so upset about the idea of my talking to one of her friends, but the more I watched her, the more she shut down. "What's wrong?" I reached over and placed my hand on hers. I could feel her shaking, and as the silence in the car seemed to smother us she became more upset.

"Can you take me home?" she squeezed her eyes shut as a tear began to leak from the corner.

"What? Why?" I shook my head trying to figure out what had just happened.

"I just want to go home please," her voice was almost inaudible as it trembled.

"If that's really what you want," I turned into a parking lot of a local grocery store as I shifted the Explorer into park.

"It is," she swallowed and when she realized where we were and that I'd had stopped driving, she became even more panicked.

oooooooooo

Maddie

I knew this was a bad idea. My brain had been telling me not to do this for days, yet when he'd kissed me it made me second guess my resolve. Now as we drove through the city all I could think about was the fact that he knew stuff about me. He'd been checking up on me, asking my friends what I liked, and he knew where I lived.

As crazy as it sounded, this was exactly how things had started with Richard. It was slow at first, but the longer I dated him, the more he found out. After the first month of our relationship, he knew everything about me.

"What are you doing?" I swung my head around trying to take in my surroundings. We were parked in a grocery store parking lot in the far corner away from the other vehicles.

"We need to talk," Cole turned the key, so the car stopped idling and shifted in his seat.

He had a look of determination on his face as he unfastened his seatbelt, and turned to face me fully. I unclipped my seatbelt also, but instead of moving closer, I burrowed back as far as I could get away from him. I hadn't felt like this in so long, but being here with him was bringing all those feelings I'd buried so long ago right back to the surface. I felt trapped. My heart was racing, and sweat was breaking out across the back of my neck and forehead. My hands were shaking, and as I watched Cole move closer, I felt myself flatten against the door.

"What's wrong?" Cole's eyes pleaded with me. "What happened back there?"

I shook my head slowly as the buzzing in my ears softened. "I can't," I whispered.

"Can't what?" he reached out and placed his hand on my knee. I know he meant for it to be a soothing gesture, but all it did was make me retreat further. "Talk to me Maddie. Tell me what's going on in there," he pointed to my head and instead of putting his hand back on my knee he put it in his lap.

I sucked in a deep breath and blew it back out, "I told you…I'm broken." The tears that I'd been fighting to hold back rushed to the surface and began spilling down my cheeks. "I knew this was a bad idea. I knew I shouldn't have done what I said I would never do and told you no. I can't go back there…ever."

"What are you talking about?" he shook his head at me as his voice rose. I couldn't help but recoil as I turned angry eyes on him.

"You know nothing about it! You don't know what I've been through! If you did, you wouldn't want me!" I was shouting at him and getting angrier by the second, and the calm expression that he kept wasn't helping at all. If anything it made me want to slap him. "Say something!" I screamed as I turned to face him fully. He stayed impassive as he watched me shake and seethe with anger. "You wanted me to talk..." I was fuming at this point, and I really hadn't told him anything. We hadn't breached the surface of what Richard had done to me. We'd come nowhere close to any of it, and as angry as I was I still wondered if I could tell him.

When I made eye contact, all I saw was pity in his eyes. "I don't need your pity," I scowled. "Now...take me home!"

"No!" he growled. It was ominous, and even though I hadn't seen Cole get truly angry yet, I feared him.

"Please take me home," I begged. He turned to face the windshield and as I waited I watched as his knuckles turn white, and he reared back to pound on the steering wheel.

"We're going to talk damn it," his voice was low and angry. "I understand you more than you think."

"Oh yeah?" I shouted. I had a bad habit of inflaming someone more when they were angry. Richard had always used that as an excuse when he'd hit me. He'd blame me, tell me it was my fault that he reacted the way he did. He'd say that I knew exactly what to do to push his buttons.

"Yeah," Cole sighed as he hit the steering wheel again and muttered the words that I almost missed. "My dad hit me too."

"What?" I gasped as my eyes went wide.

He lifted his head and as I looked into his eyes the understanding that had been there before was now shining back at me along with pain. "The scars that you asked about…my dad did that." His shoulders slumped as he shook his head at me, "So you see…I get it."

oooooooooo

Cole

I watched her face as the words I'd just let slip out sank in. She hadn't expected it, and by the tears that were flowing freely down her face I don't know if she really knew what to say. I watched as the anger and fear she'd had melted away as she slid closer to the middle of the seat.

"I'm so sorry," she whispered as she reached over and placed her hand on my forearm. "I didn't know."

I lifted my head to stare into her eyes as I nodded slowly, "No one does. Only Wes."

She gave a quick nod as she sucked her lip into her mouth and began chewing on it. "How old were you?"

"Nine," I muttered as I looked away to stare out the driver's side window.

She gasped before replying, "It wasn't your fault. You know that right? You were just a kid."

I squeezed my eyes shut as the painful memories rose to the surface. I hadn't told anyone about my dad. Wes was the only one who knew anything, and even he didn't know the whole story. All the years of living in that house…listening to my mother cry at night…trying to take care of my little sister, and protect her from our father. What I ultimately did to stop the beatings…

"Richard didn't always hit me," she began so quietly I almost didn't hear her. I nodded, so she knew I was listening, but stayed quiet hoping she'd keep talking. "We met in college…he was three years older than me, and studying to be a lawyer. When he came up to talk to me the first time, I couldn't believe it was happening. He was charming, and good looking, and I was a nobody. He asked me out on a date that afternoon. Things progressed quickly with us, and I let it because at the time I really liked him. He always knew what to say, how to act…" she trailed off as she began twisting the hem of her shirt in her fingers. "The first time he hurt me was a month after we started dating. I'd been on the quad with some friends from class. Richard came up and was mad that some of my friends were guys. He grabbed me so hard that he left a bruise on my arm. He told me to study inside where no one could stare at me. When I showed him the bruise the next day, he apologized. He said he didn't mean to, and I shouldn't anger him. He said if I'd listened, things like that wouldn't happen. I believed him. He always found a way to make it my fault. It took me three years to leave him," she lifted her gaze to stare at me. "You wonder why I act like I do? It's because I can never go back to that."

"I'm not him," I reached up to cup her cheek. "I would never hit you. Never!"

"I don't know if I'll ever be able to trust you…you see? I'm broken," she shrugged and tried to look away.

"You're not broken. You've just had your trust broken. I wanna be with you Maddie. I wanna be the one to help you get your trust back. I'm broken too," I leaned forward to place a kiss to her forehead, and instead of pulling away she actually leaned into me.

"It's gonna take some time for me," she gave me a half smile. "Every time you do or say something that reminds me of the past, it's gonna to cause me to shut down. I can't help it. It's been my mantra for so long...*run.*"

"We can help each other," I reached up to cup her cheek. "I've got baggage too."

"Tell me," she whispered. "Tell me about your dad."

As much as I knew I needed to be open and honest with her, I couldn't. I'd never opened up about it, and I knew I wasn't ready now. "Not tonight. Another time."

"I'm sorry," she slowly bobbed her head up and down.

"Don't be...it's my past," I tried to reassure her, but she wasn't having it. Her shoulders sank even lower as she wiped at her eyes.

"No...I mean I ruined tonight," she began chewing her lip once again as she darted her eyes up to mine.

"It's ok," I smiled. "Why don't we get some takeout and eat on the beach? I think I might have a blanket back there to sit on," I pointed toward the back of the car.

"But the restaurant?" what looked like fear flitted across her face.

"It's no big deal. Plans change," I shrugged.

"Richard would never have let me change our plans," she murmured as she turned and began buckling her seatbelt.

"I'm not him," I reached over and gripped her chin. "I'm not him," I murmured again as I watched her deflate and relax for the first time in the last hour. Perhaps this was the beginning...the beginning to something, neither one of us, had been expecting nor looking for...the only question now was...was I ready?

Chapter 14

Maddie

After the explosive but enlightening conversation we'd had earlier in the evening, I wasn't sure what to expect from Cole. However, now as we sat wrapped in each other's arms on the beach staring at the waves I couldn't be more content.

Since I'd ruined Cole's plans, he'd stopped at a local diner and grabbed some burgers and fries. We shared a chocolate milkshake and were now enjoying the sounds of the waves lapping up on the sand.

"You ok now?" Cole leaned forward and whispered in my ear.

I nodded as I shifted in his arms. After we'd finished eating, I'd moved to sit between his legs. He'd wrapped his arms around me and tugged my back flush with his chest. I could feel his heart hammering away against my back, and the rhythm was quite soothing.

"I am now," I mumbled on a sigh as I continued to stare out at the water. It was peaceful sitting there in his arms. So peaceful that I almost didn't want the evening to end. I felt like we'd had such a rough start, and now as the stars began shining brightly overhead it was nearing time to leave. "It's so peaceful here," I murmured.

"I always loved the beach growing up," Cole's voice was quiet almost timid. "My mom used to bring us when we were little."

"Really?" I leaned my head to the side and rested it on Cole's bent knee.

"Yeah," he blew out a breath. "Dad hated it though. He hated everything about the beach. The sand, the sun, the noise," he almost growled.

"Tell me about it," I coaxed. I knew he had a hard time opening up. It was obvious from the very start. Every time we would come near the subject he'd change it, but now that we were here in the dark it seemed easier to get him to talk.

oooooooooo

Cole

I don't know why I felt so safe going back to that place, but here sitting on the sand with my arms around her…I felt like I could tell her anything. She was so understanding and compassionate, and the longer we sat enjoying the silence, the more I wanted her to know me.

"I don't really remember when it started, probably before I was born. I always remember my mom crying at night. She was always on edge when Dad was around, and the older I got, the more I noticed. Sometimes I'd catch her in the bathroom crying and trying to cover a bruise. I'd ask her what she was doing, and she'd make an excuse that she'd hurt herself. I was little," I shrugged against Maddie's back. "I believed her because she was my mom, she was supposed to have all the answers."

Maddie slowly turned in my arms and lifted her eyes to look at me. She scanned my face and sucked that lower lip into her mouth again. I now knew this was a nervous habit, and I waited to see what she would do next. When she didn't move to say or do anything, I continued on, "One day I caught them fighting in the kitchen. Dad was mad about Mom fixing soup for dinner. He wanted something different, and she refused to cater to him. I watched him lift his arm, and slap her across the face for it. He shouted at her, called her stupid, and then poured the soup down the drain in the sink. I can remember being so shocked that my dad would do that that I threw myself in front of her to stop him when he went to hit her again. Instead of her taking the beating that night, he hit me. I'd never been so scared in my life. He yelled at me for getting in the way, and then he dragged me upstairs." I watched as Maddie shrunk down in my lap. Based on the reaction, I guessed that something similar had happened to her. "He tossed me down on my bed and then yanked his belt from the belt loops of his dress pants." I shook my head as the memory played over in my mind like a movie. It was still vivid as if it had happened yesterday. "That was the first of many. By the time, Angela was born I was taking a beating at least every other day. As much as I loathed being around him, knowing that it was me instead of my sister, or mom helped some."

"Oh my god!" Maddie gasped. "I'm sorry," she whimpered slightly as she sucked her tears back. I could tell that my past was effecting her even though she was trying to not let it.

"Don't be," I slowly shook my head as I lifted my gaze to the sky. "He's dead," I let the words slip out. "He can't hurt me anymore," I turned back to look at her as I lifted my hands to cup her face. I let my thumbs trail over her cheeks wiping away the tears as I stared deep into her eyes. "We're not so different...you and I." Before she could respond, I dipped my chin and captured her lips in a sweet kiss. Maddie was just the balm my soul needed. Even though I couldn't tell her about my darkest secret, letting her in even this much had helped. As our lips moved together, taking comfort in the bond we were building, I could feel my broken soul slowly fusing back together. Every little crack, break, and splinter was slowly fusing as Maddie's heart began to heal them.

oooooooooo

Maddie

I couldn't believe what I was hearing. How could a parent let someone do something like that to their child? How could his mother not protect him? He was just a kid, and she let him protect her. My heart hurt as I watched the sadness fill Cole's eyes. He'd gone from this strong, fearless man to a scared little boy in just a short amount of time. Watching him stare at me like he was waiting for me to reject him was causing my heart to squeeze in my chest.

"It wasn't your fault," I licked my lips as I peered up at him. "None of it…whatever happened in that house, you didn't cause it." I hoped he understood what I was trying to say. I hoped that he realized how much I was like him, and I hoped that whatever was happening in that moment was the beginning of something good. We both needed someone to heal us. Someone who could fill that black hole that was left by our past.

"Maddie?" I could hear the unspoken question in his voice as his eyes pleaded for permission. I nodded, and within a split second Cole crushed his mouth to mine. Where the last kiss had been soft and sweet, this one was bruising and desperate. It was as if he thought I was going to run away. He kept his hands on my cheeks holding me in place as he slanted his head, and plunged his tongue deep into my mouth.

The onslaught of euphoria was instantaneous, and I felt a rush of adrenaline run through me. Goose bumps rose on my arms and legs, and heat pool between my legs. I'd been holding back so long, afraid to feel again, afraid to let anyone in, but more importantly afraid of letting a man in, so much so that I couldn't control the rush of feelings my body was currently experiencing. Cole was tearing the bricks away one-by-one. The wall that I'd built between us when I'd first met him was crumbling faster than either of us knew.

As his hands left my face to slide down to my shoulders, and then to wrap around me, I turned in his arms and pressed my chest to his. A moan I didn't know I was holding in bubbled up inside me as I slid my arms around his shoulders and began tangling my fingers in his soft hair. "Maddie," he gasped when he broke the kiss "You're so beautiful. Tell me you feel what I feel," he begged as he moved to kiss my jaw. Before I could respond, I felt his lips make contact with the scar I'd been hiding for years. My makeup covered it, and unless he really looked hard, Cole wouldn't even know it was there. As his lips skimmed across it, I couldn't help but freeze. It was a natural reaction for me, and I only hoped Cole didn't pick up on it.

"What's wrong?" his breathed right next to my ear.

"Nothing," I gasped as he tugged on the lobe with his teeth.

"I felt it Maddie. You stiffened...why?" he pulled back to look at me, and what I saw brought the tears back. He wasn't angry or upset like I'd thought he would be, and he was patient and curious.

"Richard cut me there," I whispered. "I don't like to be touched there."

Cole swallowed as he stared at me, "That bastard didn't deserve you." He reached up to caress my jaw, "I promise…no one will ever touch you again."

Whatever restraint I'd been using to keep myself in check that evening had just been obliterated with those simple words coming from him. No one had ever offered me protection. Richard had always had everyone believing him, and now Cole was offering the one thing that had seemed unreachable all those years ago. As he studied me, waiting to see what I would do, I launched myself at him catching him completely off guard.

When I crashed into his chest, we toppled backwards on the blanket. Cole grunted slightly as his back hit the sand, and I landed in a pile of uncoordinated limbs on top of him. Before I could talk myself out of it, I sealed my mouth to his and resumed our feverish kiss. Cole's arms banded around me holding me in place on top of him. One palm went to my hip, and the other buried itself in my hair.

"Maddie? What are you doing?" he panted as I shifted on top of him. I could feel his cock hardening under me and based on his strained voice knew he was currently hanging onto his sanity by a thread.

"Don't think, feel," I mumbled against his lips as I deepened the kiss, and began sliding my hand slowly down the front of him. I don't know what happened to cause me to stop holding back...him understanding me...attraction that I'd been fighting since we met...desire to feel alive again? Cole stirred something in me that made me wanting more. I'd been denying it for weeks, telling myself that I couldn't have it that he wouldn't understand, but he does. He understands more than I ever thought possible.

My right hand continued its descent until I felt him, rock hard and pulsing through the denim. I broke the kiss and lifted my head to look into his hooded eyes as I squeezed lightly. He groaned and closed his tight as a mumbled curse escaped his lips. When I went to shift myself again, Cole took the opportunity to roll us. I gasped from being taken by surprise but soon recovered when he moved to cover me. One muscular thigh went between my legs as a knee slid up and brushed the juncture between them.

My head tried to roll to the side as I felt him lean forward and capture mouth again. This was getting hot and heavy fast. Did I want this? Was I even ready for something like this? Even if I was, did I want to be out here on the beach where anyone could see?

"Tell me stop," Cole panted as he rolled hips creating friction right where I needed it. "Maddie," he kissed right below my ear "please tell me to stop."

Right at that moment my brain decided to check in and tell me this was a bad idea. I quickly released my fists where they were grasping his shirt, and pushed lightly on his chest, "Stop! Please stop!" I shoved a little harder.

Cole released his hold on me and rolled to the side. He flung an arm over his face covering his eyes as he tried to get his breathing back under control. My entire body began trembling. It was almost as if it remembered what it was like to fight off Richard.

"I'm sorry," I heard him mumble, and I turned my head to the side to face him. "I didn't mean for that to happen."

"It was just as much my fault," tears pooled in my eyes and I slammed my hands in the sand beside me in anger.

"What's wrong?" Cole lifted himself to a sitting position.

I shook my head as I turned away, "It's not you."

"Then what?" he reached out and placed his hand on my shoulder. I flinched at the contact causing him to withdraw.

"It's him isn't it? What did he do to you?" he begged as he waited patiently.

"All kinds of stuff, but he never stopped when I asked him to," I murmured. "Not once."

"Maddie," he tentatively called. "Look at me, please?"

When I turned to face him, he had his eyes downcast. He lifted his gaze as a sadness filled it, "I'll never force you to do anything you don't want to do. No matter what. Do you understand me?"

I nodded. I wanted to believe him, and at the moment I did, simply because I'd just asked him to stop, and he did.

"I do want to be with you, but not here," he waved his arms around. "When we get there, it will be somewhere private where I can have you all to myself."

I could feel my face heating as he smirked at me, and I hoped that he couldn't see it in the dark.

"It's getting late...you ready to head back home?" he stood and offered his hand.

"Yeah...I've got an early morning tomorrow," I sighed as he helped me up.

As I stood beside him, Cole folded the blanket we'd been sitting on, and then wrapped his arm around me and guided me back to where we'd parked. I knew that tonight signified a huge step in the healing process, and even though I'd stopped things I'd still made a giant step forward. Cole Walker was slowly cementing my broken pieces back together one date at a time.

Chapter 15

Maddie

"So how was your date?" Erin nudged me in the side as we made our way to the back of the coffee shop. We'd been to a meeting, and decided to catch up after. With work, and going to the gym we really hadn't seen each other much over the past several days.

"It was good," I smiled softly as I thought back to how sweet Cole had been.

"Just good?" she wrinkled her nose at me. "I would think a man like him would be better than good. What aren't you telling me?"

"Nothing," I avoided looking her in the eyes as I sipped my coffee. "We grabbed some burgers and ate on the beach."

"Maddie, I can tell something happened by the way you're stalling. Now spill!"

"I told him..." I trailed off. "About Richard."

"And?" Erin turned to face me fully as we sat on the couch in the back of the shop.

"And nothing," I shrugged non-committaly.

"Maddie?" she narrowed her eyes.

"Fine!" I growled. "I had a meltdown. Are you happy now?"

"No," she whispered. "What did he do?"

"Nothing," I sipped my coffee again. I was trying to avoid telling her about Cole. I didn't think he'd want me spreading his secrets, but she was really digging today.

"Are you going out again?" she grinned.

"He wants to go to the movies Friday night," I glanced around scanning the coffee shop. It was still a habit to search for Richard. I hadn't run into him yet in all the times Erin, and I had been here, but I still wasn't able to relax. I just knew my luck would run out one day.

"Oooh," she smirked. "Dark theater with a hot guy...where can I sign up?"

"You're too much," I shook my head at her as I finished off my coffee and set the empty cup on the table beside us. "So what have you been up too lately? I feel bad that we don't get to talk more."

"Not much," she sighed. "I've been going to the self-defense class. Do you think you'll come back?"

"Maybe," I murmured. I hadn't told Erin that Cole had been giving me private lessons on a daily basis, and now I felt guilty. I wasn't sure why, but it was like I was hiding something from her. "I'll think about it."

"Do you think Wes is single?" she blurted out.

"Uh...I don't know," I couldn't figure out why she was asking me.

"Do you think you could ask Cole the next time you see him?" she was flushing bright red right before my eyes but she forged on. "He's hot, and with the way he moves around that gym I'm sure he could bring a woman to her knees."

"Erin!" I gasped. "What's gotten into you?"

She shrugged, "I haven't gotten laid in months."

I shook my head as a laugh burst out, "Why don't you come with me to the gym today afternoon and ask him yourself?"

"What are you doing there today?" her forehead wrinkled as she studied me.

"Cole's been teaching me privately. I'm sorry I didn't tell you sooner," I chewed on the inside of my mouth while I waited for a reaction.

Instead of being upset, she grinned at me, "I'll come today. Maybe he can teach me too." When she saw my face fall, she shoved me lightly, "I'm kidding…about the teaching. I'll come with you though."

"Meet me there at four?" I stood from the couch I'd been perched on. "I have to get home."

"Sure…today at four. I'll be there," she grinned and snapped her head in a quick nod.

ooooooooo

Cole

It had been three days since our date. Three days of convincing myself that the feelings I was having were deeper than lust. I don't know what it was about her, but just being around her made the world seem brighter. The more I thought about her, the more I wanted her, and the waiting for Friday to come was killing me.

"Dude," Wes shoved me in the shoulder. "Wake up!"

I turned to face him and scowled, "I am awake."

"Well, you're not here," he waved his arms around. "If you're going to spot me, you need to be here. I don't want to die from dropping a bar on my neck." He moved to sit on the weight bench and laid back.

"Yeah, yeah," I sighed. "I'm not gonna let you die. Who else would try to boss me around if you weren't here?" I smirked as I helped him lift the bar loaded down with weights above his chest.

"What do you mean try?" he grunted as he extended his arms forcing the weight into the air.

"I mean…you do think you tell me what to do," I rolled my eyes at him as he blew out a breath and placed the bar back on the rack.

"You quittin' already? That was only one. You turnin' soft on me?" I taunted. I knew I was getting to him I just wasn't sure how far I could push it today. We'd been going around like this for two days, and I could tell I was getting on his last nerve.

"I'm no pussy," he growled. "You're the pussy, pussy," he stood and began stalking towards the ring. He grabbed his gloves and mouth guard before turning on me. "Get your shit so I can beat some sense into you," he pointed to where my gym bag was piled in the corner. "I'll show you who the pussy is," he grumbled as he began climbing into the ring.

After strapping my gloves on, I stretched and popped my neck a few times. We hadn't gone at it in over a week, and I was sure Wes had been itching to get me in this position. "Maddie's coming by tonight so stay away from my face," I commanded as I pointed at him and climbed in.

"You worried I might improve it," he taunted.

"You're a dead man," I grumbled as I walked forward and bumped my gloved fists to his.

Before I could step back, Wes took a swing. I ducked before rearing back out of the way. He wasn't playing around tonight, and if I didn't stay on top of my game, I was going to have some nice bruises tomorrow. I chuckled to myself as I waited patiently to make my move. I didn't often swing , but when I did, I didn't miss. Just as my left hand came forward, I swiped my leg out causing him to trip and stumbled back.

"Playing dirty I see," he grumbled. "You trying to show off for your girl?"

At the mention of Maddie, I swung my head towards the door. Just as my eyes connected with hers, a look of horror flashed across her. Within seconds, I was stumbling back from the blow Wes had just inflicted on my head. I whipped my gaze back to him as I righted myself.

"You fucker," I growled. "Now who's playing dirty?" I advanced with both arms swinging as I took shots at his ribs causing him to curl into a ball. He backed up until he was against the ropes before dropping to the ground.

"Dude," he spit his guard out as he shook his head. "I was joking around."

"She's not something to joke about," I lifted my arm and used it to wipe the sweat that was now beading on my forehead off.

"Sorry," he placed his hands on his knees as he tried to recover. "Why don't we finish this later? You need to calm down…maybe get laid?" he grinned as he climbed out of the ring and headed in the direction of where he'd left his water bottle.

"Whatever," I grumbled. "Now who's the pussy?"

He didn't respond as he continued to walk away, and in a way it was probably a good thing. He was right...I was sexually frustrated at the moment. It had been more than a month since I'd been with anyone, and I had no idea when Maddie would give the ok to take things further. Normally I didn't worry about things like getting laid, but with Maddie I wanted it to mean something.

"Hey," I smiled as I walked over to where she was leaning against the wall with her friend Erin.

"Hey," she smiled back and pushed herself to an upright position. "Everything ok?"

"Now it is," I gave her the smile that most women found irresistible. "You're here...everything's great now."

"Cole," she blushed as she wrapped her arms around her middle. "Don't say stuff like that."

"Why?" I moved closer, so we were almost touching. "It's true."

She closed her eyes and inhaled deeply before letting them open to gaze up at me, "You seem tense."

"I'm fine. Wes just needs a good ass kicking," I shrugged but kept myself planted in front of her. I was caught off guard by the change in direction of the conversation, but didn't want to back off just yet. "I'm glad you came today...wanna work on some more moves or are you going to do your own thing?"

"Um..." she glanced at Erin before looking back to me and shrugging. "Don't really have a plan."

I was so absorbed in the moment that I didn't even notice Wes come up beside me, but as I went to speak, I was suddenly jolted forward by a smack to the back of the head. I turned my head and narrowed my eyes on him. "What the hell was that for?"

"Stop flirting and start working," he pointed to the mats where we usually did our workouts.

"Mind your own business shithead," I placed my arm on the wall beside me to brace myself. The last thing I wanted was to fall on top of Maddie or Erin because Wes had decided to be a teenager today.

ooooooooo

Maddie

"Hey," Wes smiled at Erin. "You wanna get some private lessons since these two are too busy eye fucking each other to do anything?"

"Sure," Erin giggled before she turned to look at me. "Sorry," she bit her lip. "I'm going with him."

"That's fine," I laughed. I knew when she had agreed to come with me today it was so she could be near him. Now I didn't feel so bad wanting be with Cole.

"So," Cole turned back to face me as I watched Erin bounce off behind Wes. "We gonna do this or what?"

"I'm game," I smiled as I waited for him to back up and let me pass. When he didn't, I placed my hand on his chest and pushed lightly. "You gonna let me by?"

"No," he whispered as he tipped his chin down. The hairs around my ear tickled my face where his breath stirred them.

"Cole?" I could feel my voice quiver, and I wasn't sure if it was from desire or fear. I didn't like feeling trapped, but Cole made me feel something else too. In a weird way, he made me want to be trapped by him. "I can't get to the mats if you don't move."

"Maybe I don't want to move yet," he continued to talk quietly to me as he shuffled forward causing me to step back and press myself into the wall beside us. "Maddie you make feel things that I've never felt before. My brain is telling me to slow down, but my body is begging me to get closer. I know you wanna wait, but I want you to know what you do to me. Do you feel that?" he rolled his hips forward letting the bulge in his shorts skim across my thighs. I watched with rapt attention as he squeezed his eyes shut before letting his head fall forward and rest on the wall above my shoulder. "I've never felt this strongly about a woman before," he muttered. "You've completely consumed me."

"I know what you mean," I whispered so quietly I wasn't sure he heard me. "I feel things too."

"What are you doing to me?" he groaned as he pushed off the wall and shook his head lightly.

"I've asked myself that same question every morning when I wake up. I don't have an answer. I think we just need to take it day-by-day," I smiled at him as I turned to head towards the mats. "You coming? I need to kick some ass today," I winked as I watched him adjust his shorts.

"Yeah...I need someone to kick my ass, so we're a good match," he chuckled as he tugged his gloves back on and followed me to the mat.

I wasn't sure what I felt when I left the gym that day. Exhaustion? Happiness? Desire? Lust? I didn't think it could be love, but I knew it was something. Cole had burrowed his way into my heart, and each day he got a little deeper. I smiled to myself as I climbed into my car. Friday's date couldn't get here fast enough. The more time I spent with Cole, the more I wanted to be with him. He was shining a light in my life that I didn't even know existed anymore, and because of it I was off my usual game. I'd always been aware in the past of anyone around me, and if I'd been paying attention instead daydreaming when I left the gym that night I would have notice the black Mercedes parked across the street and the feeling of dread that tried to settle in the pit of my stomach. I'd pushed it aside instead of listening to it, and I've been kicking myself ever since.

Chapter 16

Maddie

"Rough day?" Cole glanced over at me. We were driving through town on our way to the movies. It had been a long day, and I'd had to put down a dog this afternoon.

"You could say that," I sighed. "Mrs. Thompson came in today with her Lab, Cookie. He's been sick for a while, and today I had to put him down. I know it's my job, but it's hard ya know. It doesn't matter how many times you do it, it never gets easy."

"I'm sorry," Cole mumbled as he reached over and grabbed my hand. After lacing our fingers together, he lifted our joined hands and kissed the back of mine.

"I'll get past it. It just takes time," I turned my gaze out the window, and began watching the buildings pass by us as we headed towards the far end of town.

"Anything new happen today?" he smiled when he glanced at me.

"If you mean Jo bugging me, then yes," I groaned just thinking back to the conversation we'd had this morning. Jo had come barging into an exam room yammering on about going out next week. She'd said that she and Ben had made plans and that I had to come. "They want to go to Vibe on Wednesday," I bit down on my lip as I chanced a look in his direction. We hadn't made any plans yet, and I wasn't sure if we were at that stage where we could plan dates without asking yet.

"Ok," Cole shrugged as he turned the Explorer into the movie theater parking lot.

"How do you know I was inviting you?" I tried to hold back the smile that pulled at the corners of my mouth.

"You don't want me too? I just thought..." he trailed off, and the look on his face made me give in.

"I'm kidding. I just didn't think you'd want to go," I giggled as I watched him sag in relief. "You don't seem like the kinda guy who takes no for an answer anyway."

"I'm not, but with you everything's different. I never know what to do, or how things will work out. I'm trying just to let them happen," he shrugged as he released my hand and climbed out of his side. He rounded the front, and stopped by my door to open it. After helping me out, he grabbed my hand, and began leading me to the doors of the theater. "You look beautiful tonight, by the way."

"Uh, thanks," I glanced down at the jeans I was wearing. I'd changed three times before Cole had picked me up, and I didn't think I looked that great. Jeans and a simple blouse weren't all that fancy.

"Would you stop?" he paused at the door, and turned to face me. "You seem always to worry about everyone else's opinion and not your own. I know he messed with your head for a long time, but you are beautiful, and you need to believe that."

"I'm just not used to hearing it, that's all," I whispered. "Thank you."

"You're welcome. Now...you ready?" he pushed the door open, and stepped back to let me pass.

When we entered, the smell of popcorn and chocolate filled the air. It had been years since I'd been to the movies. Richard had never wanted to go, and after I'd left him I'd been too afraid to be anywhere dark by myself.

"You've got a goofy grin on your face," Cole nudged me as the line moved forward.

"I love the movies. I don't remember the last one I saw in the theater though. It's been forever," I leaned into him feeling content.

"It can't have been that long," he cocked his head to the side as he smiled down at me.

"Well..." I thought for a minute "the last movie I saw was before..." I trailed off. "So it's been at least eight years."

"What?" Cole's eyes went wide. "That's crazy!"

"You wouldn't understand," I grumbled. "No one ever does," I released his hand and crossed my arms over my chest. I was feeling defensive, and beginning to wonder if I should have just kept my mouth shut.

"I'm sorry. I shouldn't have said that," Cole murmured as he wrapped an arm around my shoulders. At this point, the line had moved, and it was our turn to purchase tickets. "What do you want to see?" he glanced at me waiting.

"You want me to pick? I thought we were coming to see Street Fight 4?" I wrinkled my forehead as I looked up at him.

"That was the plan...and then you said you hadn't been to the movies in eight years. So...I think you should get to pick what you want to see," he reached in to his back pocket and pulled out his wallet.

"Um..." I looked up at the sign above the ticket counter. There were several movies out that I wanted to see, but I wasn't sure what Cole would like. I didn't want to make him sit through a love story, but I really wasn't in the mood for action either.

"You want to see The Cove, don't you?" he grinned down at me.

"But you don't," I muttered.

"Two for The Cove," he pushed a twenty across the counter to the girl selling the tickets.

"What?" my head snapped up. "Really we don't have to see that."

"Oh, you'll love it," the girl smiled at me as she handed our tickets to Cole. "Shawn Dawson is so hot," she grinned at me before blushing at Cole.

"See," Cole chuckled. "He's soooo hot," he fanned himself as he grabbed the tickets and led me towards the snack counter.

"You didn't have to do that," I mumbled.

"I wanted to…besides…I don't plan on watching the movie," he murmured so quietly I almost missed it.

"Cole," I scolded.

"What? You can't expect me to watch the movie when I've got you sitting beside me in those sexy jeans."

"We're adults," I hissed.

"And it's dark," he added with a smirk.

ooooooooo

Once we'd gotten our snacks, a large diet soda to share and a giant bucket of popcorn, Cole led us into the theater. It wasn't dark yet, and very few people were inside. I glanced around, not sure where he'd want to sit. Anytime I had gone anywhere with Richard, I'd never been allowed to have an opinion, so with Cole this was a new concept for me. It didn't matter that

~ 184 ~

Richard wasn't part of my life anymore, every decision I made was as if he still was. I wasn't used to this independence, and as I stood there scanning the rows of seats in confusion Cole nudged me from behind.

"How about here?" he moved down a row that was just a few from the back.

"Sure," I followed him to the center where he plopped down and lifted the armrest that was between the seats creating a loveseat for us.

"You ok?" he leaned forward to set our soda on the floor.

"Yeah," I looked around again. "I'm just...I don't know. Ignore me," I muttered.

"No, what's wrong?" he turned slightly, and right at that moment the lights began to dim.

"This is just different for me, that's all. I promise...I'm fine," I whispered as I leaned in to him, and made myself comfortable. I felt Cole relax as he accepted my answer, and as the previews began to roll, I found myself getting lost in the moment.

oooooooooo

Cole

I didn't really know what was going on with this movie. I tried to pay attention, but with Maddie

~ 185 ~

sitting there snuggled into my side wearing those skin tight jeans I couldn't think of anything other than touching her. Every once in a while, I felt her sigh, or saw her wipe at her eyes, but other than that she's been lost in the story. The ticket girl was right. Maddie was loving this.

I knew I probably should have left her alone since she hadn't been to a movie in so long, but I couldn't. My body was humming it was so keyed up right then, and having her hand on my thigh so close to where I wanted it to be was causing me to die a little more with every passing second. I wasn't sure how far I could push her tonight, but when she snuggled a little deeper into my side, I knew I needed to try something.

"You're killing me," I murmured into her hair as I let my arm drop down around her back, and pull her closer to my side. She tensed slightly but didn't pull away. Instead, she turned sideways and draped her legs across my lap. When her denim-clad thighs brushed over my semi-hard cock, I groaned. This was not fair.

She broke her stare down with the movie screen and turned towards me as a coy smile slipped into place. Who was this, and where was the Maddie that came with me tonight? Before I could react, she slide closer, and placed an open palm on my chest as she leaned up and pressed her mouth to mine, "This is what you wanted...right?" she whispered against my lips.

"You don't have to do this," I pulled back as I watched a frown appear on her beautiful face.

"I want to," she moved closer, and this time I didn't hold back.

When her lips covered mine I responded by wrapping my arms tighter around her, and pulling her flush to my chest. She gasped, and I tentatively slipped my tongue in to taste her. It had been a week since I'd kissed her like this, and the taste I'd gotten on the beach hadn't been enough.

She was slow to respond at first, but when I didn't push to deepen our contact, she soon melted for me. Her hands went from being idle, to wrapping around my neck, and tangling in the hair at the base of my neck. I groaned when she tugged lightly. This woman knew exactly what to do to unravel me, and she was great at it.

I could feel her chest rising quickly as her breath quickened, and she gripped me tighter as if I might disappear. "Maddie?" I gasped. "You ok?" I pulled back to look into her eyes and what I saw caused me to groan again. The fear that had once possessed them was gone, and all I saw now was trust. She was finally giving in fully to whatever was going on between us. Acceptance was there along with want, and several other emotions that I couldn't quite place.

When she leaned in to resume the kiss, I let my hand slide up her thigh slowly, and make its way around to her backside where I squeezed lightly. She responded by grinding herself into my lap even further, and I knew at that moment if we didn't stop we'd be doing it right there in the theater.

"Maddie?" I panted as I broken the kiss again. I wanted to make sure that she wanted the same thing I wanted and that I wasn't pushing her into something that she wasn't ready for.

She nodded before clarifying, "I want you too."

It didn't take me any more convincing as I lifted her off my lap, grabbed her hand, and began tugging her along behind me as I stalked toward the exit. "The movie isn't over," she giggled from behind me as we burst through the doors and into the lobby.

"Fuck the movie," I growled. "I'll buy you the Blu-ray."

ooooooooo

Maddie

I'd never seen him like this...all alpha and flustered. It was as if I'd lit a stick of dynamite, and I was watching the fuse slowly disappear. Cole was moving so fast towards the parking lot that I was almost running to keep up. When we got to the Explorer, he spun me, pushed my into the passenger side door before pressing the length of his body into me, and pressing a fiery kiss to my lips. "Are you sure?" he squeezed his eyes shut as if he was in pain. "I mean...we can wait, but..." he trailed off.

"I'm sure," leaned forward and nipped at his ear. "I wanna be with you Cole. I trust you. I know you won't hurt me."

"No one is ever going to hurt you again," he growled as he reached up and cupped my cheek. "I promise."

"I believe you," I reassured him.

"You're amazing...you know that?" he smiled softly at me. "You're strong, and beautiful, and smart. Any man that didn't treat you like a princess should be shot."

I could feel the tears coming, and sunk my teeth into my lip to stop them, "Thanks. You're pretty amazing yourself."

"I'm lucky...that's what I am," he sighed as he stepped back, opened my door, and helped me climb in. I watched him bound around the front, before climbing into his own seat, and cranking the car. "My place or yours?"

"It' doesn't matter to me. I have to work tomorrow," I could feel my face heating. Was I really about to do this? I was just thankful that it was dark out, and it would hide my embarrassment.

"My place then...its closer," he muttered. "Buckle up," he winked at me. "I don't plan on going slow."

I swallowed not really knowing if he was talking about the driving or what was inevitably going to occur tonight once we got to his place. As soon as my belt clicked into place, Cole peeled out of the parking lot on a mission. I was really going to do this. I was going to finally let Cole in, in a way, I hadn't let anyone since Richard. Excitement, desire, and a slight fear began churning in my stomach. Richard had always told me I was a lousy girlfriend. Would Cole think differently of me after tonight? Would he even want me anymore?

Chapter 17

Cole

When I pulled into the parking lot of my building, I quickly found a spot and cut the engine. I looked over at Maddie and couldn't help but smile. She was twisting her hands together in her lap, and chewing on the inside of her cheek so hard I thought she might draw blood. I took a deep breath to calm myself, and then shoved my door open. As I rounded the back of the Explorer, I paused for a minute out of her line of sight. I needed to calm down. I wanted tonight to mean something for us. This was not some quick fuck or one night stand…this was Maddie…MY Maddie. "Did I really just say that?" I had muttered before I moved to open her door.

When I opened it, she was staring straight ahead and bouncing one of her legs vigorously. "Are you ok?" I murmured as I reached out to cup her cheek. She turned in my direction and nodded, but didn't move to get out of the car.

"You'll tell me, right?" it was a strangled whisper like she had a knot in her throat.

"Tell you what?" I cocked my head as I studied her.

"If…" she trailed off and squeezed her eyes shut.

"I don't understand," I leaned forward and pressed my forehead to hers. "Tell me what's wrong…please?"

"It's just," she swallowed. "Why is this so hard?" she muttered angrily before she took a deep breath. "It's been a long time, and Richard used to say," she began forcing the words out as she pinched her eyes shut.

I knew whatever was getting ready to fly out of her mouth was not something important. It was some lie that bastard had fed her so many times that she now believed it. Without thinking, I pressed my mouth to hers silencing her. Maddie's eyes flew open in surprise as she tried to pull back. I slid my hand from her jaw up to cup the back of her head, and hold her in place. When she finally relaxed, I broke the kiss and whispered, "Whatever he told you is wrong. You are beautiful and sexy, and I can't wait to get you out of these," I ran my other hand up her jean-clad thighs. "Relax, and if you don't want to do this, we don't have to."

"No, I want to. I just don't want to disappoint you," her eyes softened as she stared at me.

"You won't...trust me," I stepped back and offered her my hand to help her to her feet. "Come on before I embarrass myself out here," I pointed down to the obvious bulge in my pants. It was painful at this point, and when Maddie glanced down and blushed, he took notice immediately and throbbed in response.

She giggled as she slid from the seat and let me lead her to my door. After fumbling slightly with the keys, I shoved the door open, and stepped aside to allow her to enter first.

ooooooooo

Maddie

Cole's apartment was nothing like I thought it would be. It was very modern. Lots of glass and metal with nothing out of place except a

~ 193 ~

few magazines that were piled on an end table. There was a couch on the far wall that faced an entertainment center on one end of the room, and a weight bench on the other. The walls were a cream color, and the entire room had wooden floors. A large area rug was in the center under the coffee table, and an open kitchen was to the right.

As I stood there admiring the place, Cole stepped around me and tossed his keys onto the bar. The clinking noise brought me back to the present, and caused me to jump slightly.

"Relax," he murmured as he moved behind me, and wrapped his arms around my middle. "There's no rush here."

"Your place is nice," my voice hitched slightly and I couldn't figure out if it were nerves or desire to cause it.

"It's ok," he mumbled as he placed a kiss to the side of my neck.

When he hit that sensitive spot, it caused me to melt into him, and my legs began to weaken. I slowly turned in his arms, and lifted mine to wrap around his neck, "Cole?" I peered up at him hoping he understood what I was trying to say. "I'm ok," I lifted onto my tiptoes and pressed my mouth to his. "It's ok," I mumbled against his lips.

"Really? Because I'm holding on by a thread right now," he groaned.

"Really," I pressed my hips into his and caused both of us to moan in unison.

Before I could react, Cole reached down and grabbed the back of my thighs in his hands and hoisted me up his body. A growl ripped from his chest as he began walking blindly towards the back of the apartment. Our lips were still fused together, and not wanting to overthink the situation resumed the hungry kiss that had started in the living room.

"You're perfect," Cole praised as he set my feet on the floor by the bed. "How the hell did I get this lucky?" He pressed his lips back to mine so quickly that I couldn't answer him. His tongue came out and took a swipe at me silently asking to take things to a place we hadn't been yet, and my body responded with a resounding yes.

I broke the kiss, grabbed to bottom of his shirt, and began pushing it up his torso. Cole reached behind himself, grabbed the material in his hand, and ripped it over his head tossing it to the floor before sealing his mouth to mine once again. Our kisses began to spiral out of control as his hands began wandering over me. It was as if he was memorizing my body, afraid he'd never see it again. I arched into him and slid my hands over the muscles of his back. They bunched and flexed as his hands worked to free me from my shirt.

"I can't get enough of you," he groaned when he finally freed the last button of my blouse. He pushed the material off my shoulders, and stepped back to admire what was underneath. I couldn't help but feel self-conscious. Richard had been the only man to see me like this, and he'd always criticized me. What was Cole thinking at the moment?

"Beautiful," he murmured as he trailed a finger across the swell of my breasts stopping at the lace cup of my bra.

"Stop!" I blushed.

"Why?" he questioned. "You don't think you're beautiful. I obviously need to tell you so you'll start believing it. He stared at me for a minute before he stepped closer and bent down beside my ear, "He was wrong, Maddie."

I nodded silently as I reached for his belt buckle, and began to fumble with it. "Not yet," he reached down and covered my hand with his. "If you touch me, it's going to be over real quick, and I want to know what's under these first," he cupped my rear and squeezed.

"But I wanna see you," I begged as I glanced up into his eyes.

"You will," he smirked before releasing my hand, and lifting me into his arms again. I soon felt the softness of the mattress at my back as Cole placed me in the center of the bed. He made quick work of peeling me out of my jeans, and when he rocked back on his heels to admire me, I couldn't help by flush. Here I was splayed out in front of him in nothing but my pink lace bra and panties, and he was licking his lips like I was a piece of candy he couldn't wait to consume.

I stared up at him telling myself that he wasn't going to hurt me, and as I watched him stand to remove his jeans, I knew that it was the truth. His body was perfect, and as I watched his pants fall to the floor, I couldn't help the rush of desire that pooled between my legs.

"Like what you see?" he teased as he began to climb back on the bed. He moved on his hands and knees until he was hovering over me.

"Mmm hmm," I nodded as I sucked my lower lip into my mouth and began trailing my hands over his bare chest. He had a small smattering of dark hair on his pecks, but the rest was all smooth tan skin. He held himself there letting me explore at my leisure, but I could tell it was killing him. His boxers were stretched from the erection he was sporting, and it was twitching every time I touched him. His thighs were rooted on each side of my hips, and they trembled as he fought to remain still. I gave him a coy smile and trailed my right hand down his side. When I reached his waist, I moved to cup him through his boxers. His hips jacked forward as a groan tore through him. "Maddie?" he warned. I did it again only this time I lifted my head and pressed a heated kiss to his mouth. He took the silent invitation and lowered his body to make contact with mine. With experienced hands, he quickly removed my bra and began kneading my breasts in his palms. I couldn't help but curve into him. He knew exactly how to bring maximum pleasure without the pain. Richard had always been so rough that I had fought him on things like this, but Cole…Cole was bringing nothing but pleasure with his touches.

"More," I moaned as his lips left mine and began trailing down my neck. They brushed lightly over my collarbone before latching onto my right breast. "Oh god," the words slipped out without me even knowing it, and Cole chuckled against my sensitive flesh.

"You're a greedy little thing," he teased before moving to the other breast.

As tingles began to spread over my entire body, I lifted my hips to press them against him, only Cole had other plans. He growled against my breast as his hand pressed my hips down, "Not yet."

"No more teasing," I begged. "I can't take any more teasing.

"What do you want then," he lifted his head and smirked at me. His eyes were dark and smoldering as he watched my face.

"You," I gasped as I wrapped my arms around him and tugged him flush with me. "I want you now!"

He chuckled as he gave me a quick kiss before standing to remove his boxers. When he pushed them over his hips, his erection sprung free and stood at attention as his eyes darkened even more. His abs flexed with barely restrained desire as he licked his lips and scanned my body. He leaned forward, grabbed the edges of my panties, and slid them down my thighs. The moment the cool air from the room hit me, I sucked in a breath. This was it. I was really doing this, and as much as I thought I would be scared, I wasn't. I wanted him…all of him, and as he slowly crawled back onto the bed, my body began craving his touch.

He rolled to the side slightly, opened a drawer on the bedside table, and grabbed a foil packet. After ripping it open with his teeth, he quickly sheathed himself. I couldn't help but stare as his cock jutted straight out wanting me. I'd never felt desired before, and it was obvious that Cole desired me.

Once he was finished, he leaned forward and covered my body with his once again. The warm heat was as much comforting as it was a turn on. His knee burrowed between my legs as his lips sealed over mine. I couldn't help but let my eyes roll back as his fingers dipped down to where his knee was and lightly ran across the sensitive flesh. I shivered when he pressed a finger inside and swirled it around probing areas that hadn't been touched by a man in years.

"So perfect," he muttered as he dipped in again stretching me. He shifted his weight, and aligned our bodies before breaking the kiss to stare deep into my eyes. "I'm gonna try to go slow, but I don't know if I can."

"It's ok," I reassured him as I rocked my hips up trying to force him to slide in deeper.

"Maddie?" his voice was strained as he pushed forward. It had been so long since I'd had sex that I winced slightly as my body stretched to accommodate him. Cole was large. Larger than Richard, and with the time that had passed since I'd last had sex didn't help.

"You're so tight," he ground out as he paused and let me relax.

"I'm ok. Keep going," I coaxed as I wrapped my arms around his waist and tugged at his hips. I pressed my mouth to his and opened allowing his tongue to plunge in. Cole responded willingly as he rocked his hips forward causing himself finally to sink in completely. When I tighten my grip on him, he finally accepted that I was ok and began moving.

"Oh, fuck you feel good," he growled as his hips began to piston into me. It was like no experience I'd ever had. Cole knew exactly what to do to bring pleasure to the encounter. With Richard, it had always been about him. Whether he got off or was enjoying what was happening. He chose the when, where, and how. With Cole...he was making it about me.

His arms flexed as he hovered over me, his eyes pinched shut in pleasure. His lips slightly parted as he rocked forward. I reached up and ran my palms lightly down his chest admiring the way the muscles bunched and jerked under my touch.

"Cole? Oh god," I gasped when his hand left the spot where it had been perched by my hip to rub circles on my clit.

"Come on Maddie…let go. I want see what you look like when you come for me," he growled as he increased the pressure.

"Cole?" I panted as my entire body jerked and quivered as the mindless pleasure started at my toes and rushed up my body consuming everything in its wake.

"That's it," he coaxed. "Let go!"

Every muscle inside me tightened as he sped up and squeezed his eyes shut. With one last thrust of his hips, Cole released a feral growl as his entire body shook while he exploded. "Holy Fuck!" he roared as his cock swelled inside me. His arms gave out as he collapsed on top of me, trapping me against the mattress.

We laid there for a few minutes each coming down from our individual highs before he lifted himself off of me. He rolled to the side, removed the condom, and tossed it in the wastebasket beside the bed. "You ok?" he turned his head to the side and stared at me.

I nodded without answering as I rushed to pull the covers over my naked body. "Don't," he clasped his hand over mine. "You're beautiful, don't be embarrassed."

"I'm not," I shook my head. I wasn't so much embarrassed as I was nervous. The heat of the moment was over, and now reality was slowly sinking back in. The scars on my body that were usually hidden by clothes were now on full display, and I wasn't sure I was ready to explain all of them. Richard had always told me that no one would want me that way. For years, I'd believed him, but now after sharing what had just happened with Cole, I wasn't so sure anymore.

"Will you stay the night?" he propped himself up on his elbow. "I'll take you home in the morning with plenty of time to get to work," his eyes pleaded with me, and as much as I wanted to hide at the moment, I just couldn't.

I nodded slowly as I watched a smile tug at his lips, "I'll stay."

"Come here," Cole stretched out an arm beckoning me into his embrace, and I went willingly. He pulled the covers up to wrap them around us as we snuggled together in the darkness. "I don't know what's happening here, but I like it," he murmured.

"Me too," I yawned as I burrowed deeper into his side. I closed my eyes and let exhaustion over take me, but not before hearing his whispered confession. "I think I'm falling in love with you." It was quiet, and not meant for my ears. I knew he thought I was sleeping, and that's why he said it. I knew it might be awhile before he told me if ever. We were both fighting demons, and Cole's seemed to be buried deeper than mine. Who knew if I'd ever get him to open up, but after what we just shared I hoped it meant we were on the path to finding peace with each other.

Chapter 18

Maddie

For the first time in years, I actually slept all night and didn't dream. The nightmares that had plagued me for longer than I could remember didn't creep in like they usually did. At first I thought it might have been the fact that I was exhausted, but then I remembered where I was. The warm body at my back shifted and groaned before settling back down into sleep.

I rolled over just as Cole was getting comfortable, and noticed the sheet that had been bunched at his waist had slid down exposing his erection. I couldn't help but stare.

He was beautiful, every part of him, and watching him in this relaxed state was like a dream. I could stare this way, and not worry about coming across as stalkerish. His dark hair was tousled, and his jaw had a little more scruff than usually. One arm was tossed above his head, and the other was lying across this middle. As I laid there, his nose scrunched up as his lips pursed. I figured he must have been dreaming about something, but I didn't want to wake him. I lifted myself up on my elbow careful not to rock the bed, and glanced at the alarm clock on the other side of the room. It was only six a.m. I didn't need to be to work until nine. When I slumped back down in the bed, I slid closer to Cole's side. I could look, right? He shouldn't mind if I didn't wake him. Mornings with Richard came flooding back the longer I laid there. I couldn't remember how many times I'd been hit because I woke him up when he wanted to sleep late, or I forgot to wake him when he had a meeting. It seemed that most mornings I was nursing an injury of some sort for a reason that I didn't understand.

"What are you thinking about?" came a mumbled voice from beside me.

I whipped my head in Cole's direction and froze, "I'm sorry." I was starting panic. What if he got mad that I woke him?

"Sorry? Don't be," he turned his head to the side as his eyes fluttered open. When he saw my face, his expression went from playful to concern, "Hey...what's wrong?"

"Nothing," I swallowed. "I wasn't sure what to expect here. I was trying not to overthink the moment. I just wanted to enjoy this time, and here I was turning it into something entirely different.

"Do you regret last night?" he rolled onto his side, and propped himself up on his elbow.

"No," I slowly shook my head. "It's just..." I looked away. I knew it was silly. I knew I was probably driving him nuts with the way I kept bringing the past up.

As if he could read my mind, he reached up and cupped my cheek, "I'm not him," he murmured "and if I ever have the pleasure of running into him, I'm gonna beat the life out of him."

And just like that, I melted. The tension that had been radiating off of me fell away leaving nothing but what should have been there in the first-place...happiness. "I'm sorry...I'm trying...it just might take me awhile."

"It's ok," he leaned forward and pressed a kiss to my forehead. "What time do you need to be at work?"

"Nine," I smiled softly. "You?"

"I don't," he grinned. "I have the day off."

"I have to take Zeb to the dog park when I get in this morning...wanna come?" I watched is face light up, and then a smirk slid into place.

"I'll come with you," his grin broadened as he rolled and began to crawl towards me. "I'll come right now," he quickly scrambled to where I was, and had his body pressed to mine before I could react.

"You're a naughty boy," I giggled as he lowered himself, letting me feel every inch of his body against mine.

"I can be," he teased as he pressed a kiss to my neck, and then moved lower to nip at my shoulder.

"Cole?" I gasped when I felt his cock rooting around on top of the covers.

"Hmmm?" his hands began skimming down my sides, taking the sheet that was between us with them.

"I have to get cleaned up for work," I panted. My brain was saying one thing, but my body...it was craving him, and he knew it.

"Can't you be a little late?" he mumbled against my heated skin.

"No, Hannah will kill me," I pushed against his shoulders lightly causing him to look up at me.

He huffed and then sprung to a standing position, "All right. Come on." He held out his hand to help me off the bed.

"What are you doing?" I wrinkled my nose as I let him lead me into the bathroom.

"Finishing what I started and letting you bathe," he grinned as he reached into the shower, and twisted the knob.

I knew at that moment I was in for a morning I wouldn't forget. I liked this side of Cole, the playful unrestrained one, and as I followed him into the warm water, I knew I could easily get used to this.

oooooooooo

"Morning," Hannah smiled as she breezed into the office.

"Good morning," I grinned back. I was in the process of getting Zeb out of his crate to take him to the dog park. After the morning I'd spent with Cole, I was on cloud nine.

"What's got you so chipper?" Hannah stopped what she was doing and turned on me.

"Nothing," I glanced away. I was a terrible liar, and I knew if she studied my face long enough she'd figure out what I'd been doing the night before.

"Nothing huh?" she popped her hip. "You seem awfully happy for nothing. I think you met someone...am I right?"

I could feel my face heating as I felt her stare on me, "I don't know what you're talking about."

"That's fine...you don't have to tell me," she stood up straight, "but if it's that fine specimen waiting in the parking lot...well, you did good."

"I'm going to take Zeb for his exercise. I'll be back later," I scooted around her with Zeb in tow. "That's Cole, by the way."

"He's hot," Hannah called from behind me. "Better not let Jo see him. She's going to hammer you with questions when she finds out," she called after me as I pushed through the door and out into the morning sunlight.

ooooooooo

"So who's this?" Cole smiled as we began making our way over to a bench under a tree.

"This is Zeb," I smiled as I released the leash and patted Zeb on the head, signaling that he was free to go. "Hannah found him in a ditch several months ago. I've been bringing him here for exercise each day."

~ 210 ~

"Doesn't he have a home?" Cole lowered himself on the bench as he stretched his legs out in front of him.

"No," I blew out a breath. "Hannah takes him home on weekends, but she really doesn't have the space for another animal. She and her husband already have two dogs of their own, and two kids..." I trailed off.

"So where does he live?" Cole stared out across the lush grass watching Zeb roll and play in the sunshine.

"During the week...in a crate in the office," I twisted the leash in my hands and placed it on the bench beside me. "I feel bad for him, but I can't have pets where I live. I'd take him home in a heartbeat if I could. He's a sweet dog. Doesn't really bark, he's good with everybody...just had a bad run of luck of guess."

"Kinda like us huh?" Cole murmured as he shifted and lifted his arm to place it across the back of the bench.

"I guess. I never really thought of it like that," I cocked my head to the side. "He just doesn't deserve the life he was given. We're hoping to adopt him out now that he's ready."

"Ready?" Cole turned slightly, and his knee brushed against mine creating an awareness that had been hovering just below the surface since our morning in the shower.

"Yeah," I lifted my arms and shrugged lightly. "You know…ready to be around other people?"

"I haven't had a pet since I was little," Cole contemplated quietly. "You think my place is big enough?"

"What?" I gasped as I shifted to face him fully. "You want him?"

"Maybe…I haven't wanted a dog in the past, but he needs something more than what he's got."

"He's house trained," I smiled as excitement built inside me for both Cole and Zeb.

"You could help me," Cole cocked his head. "You know…if you wanted too,"

"I'll have to talk to Hannah, but I don't think it'll be a problem." I leaned in and pressed a quick kiss to his mouth, "Thank you!"

"Don't thank me yet. I have to dog proof my apartment now, and talk to my landlord. This might not go as well as you want it to."

"That's ok. Just the fact that you want us is enough for me," I smiled.

"Us?" Cole lifted his arm from where it was resting behind me and gripped the back of his neck.

"Yeah...Zeb and me," I muttered.

I watched his mouth drop open and then snap shut. "I don't know why you're having such a hard time believing this, but I'm the lucky one here. I'm waiting for you to wake up and realize that I'm not good enough for you, not the other way around," he gasped. "Any man would be lucky to have you in his life. Now...stop thinking I'm going to run. It's not happening...understand?"

"Ok," I could feel tears rising to the surface, and I blinked furiously to push them back. I was determined to be happy, and knew that accepting the way Cole saw me was a step in the right direction.

After letting Zeb have his time to run and play, Cole and I made our way back to my office. The entire walk there we discussed him adopting Zeb. I made sure to tell him that it was a process, and would take a little time on my part, but I would discuss it with Hannah that day.

When we reached the door to the animal clinic, Cole gave me a quick hug and kiss, and promised to see me later. I was planning to meet him after work at the gym. He smiled one last time at me before turning to head to his Explorer.

Once he'd gotten in and pulled out of the parking lot I turned to enter the building, but just as I placed my hand on the door, I froze. Something felt off, and I couldn't explain it. The hairs on my neck began to stand up, and I felt the stare of someone. It was almost as if I was being watched. Zeb felt it too, and when I reached down to pet his head, he lowered his ears and emitted a soft growl.

"Its ok boy," I cooed as I turned us to scan the parking lot. I didn't see anyone, but I could still feel them. Whoever they were, they were there, and they were definitely unwanted. Slowly I turned back towards the door and quickly shuffled inside. I didn't want to hang around and see who it was. My instincts had told me to run, and I was going listen.

After calming Zeb, and putting him back in his crate, I went into my office to call the local police station. I wanted to verify that my restraining order was still in effect. Richard hadn't tried to approach me in the last eighteen months, but I wouldn't put it past him.

As the phone rang, my brain began churning. What was causing me to feel this way? Was it Richard? Was he out there watching me? Was he crazy enough to try something again? Was it because I finally let Cole in? Was I in danger? As the line connected on the other end,, and I heard a voice come over all I could think was that Richard was right. I didn't deserve Cole, and he was the one out there trying to remind me.

Chapter 19

Maddie

When I left the office that afternoon, the first place I went was the gym. I was still feeling rather jumpy, and needed to be somewhere I felt safe. Still dressed in my scrubs from work, I grabbed my gym bag and burst through the doors into McKay's. I knew I must have looked crazy. When I turned to face the front desk, I watched both Cole's and Wes's heads snap up to meet mine.

"What's wrong," Cole's expression held concern and worry. "Did something happen after I left today?"

I shook my head quickly, my eyes flashing wide with panic. "Someone's watching me."

"What?" Wes rounded the desk and stalked towards the door to the gym. He shoved the doors open and burst outside. After a few a minutes, he came in scratching his head and slowly shaking it back-and-forth.

"Baby what's wrong?" Cole crept closer and wrapped me in his arms.

I was shaking from fear, and all I could do was fist his t-shirt and hold on for dear life. "I don't know," I whimpered. "Today..." I swallowed as he turned us and began walking toward the office in the front corner of the gym. He pushed open the door, led us inside, and then closed it behind us. "I just..." I couldn't quite form the words, and as Cole stood there watching me, I knew he could sense how hard this was for me.

"Take your time," he coaxed as he leaned against the edge of the desk in the room and offered me the one chair.

I nodded as I tried again, "After you left today...I got this feeling. It was like someone was there. I looked around to see if I noticed anyone, but I didn't. Zeb started growling. He never growls, ever," I glanced up at Cole as I shifted in the chair. "Anyway, I watched for a few minutes, and then I went inside. I know it's silly, but I can't help it. Someone was there."

"Come stay with me tonight," he opened his arms, and I went to stand between his legs. He wrapped me in a tight embrace and murmured against my hair, "We'll figure this out."

"You believe me?" I glanced up at him and watched the shock appear on his face.

"Why wouldn't I?" his forehead wrinkled as he watched me all the while confusion spreading across his features.

"No one ever has," I shrugged as I watched his eyes darken with anger.

"Well…that's gonna change with me. If you think someone's going to hurt you, then I intend to stop them. Now, do you want to work out tonight or just hang out? I'm not working. I was going to get a few rounds in on the speed bag and then leave."

"You can work out," I tried to smile, but my nerves were still a little raw. I wasn't sure what I was feeling at the moment…fear, happiness, or relief that he believed me.

Cole pressed a kiss to my forehead as he stood. "How did you know I was here? I mean…I know we were going to meet up here tonight, but that wasn't for a couple of hours," he scratched his head as he reached with his other hand to lace our fingers together.

"I didn't," I mumbled. "I feel safe here."

"You'll always be safe here," he reassured as he led us back out into the gym. "Never doubt that."

"I won't," I smiled at him. "You gonna lift any weights today?"

Cole shook his head slightly at my change in subject, "I wasn't planning on it, why?"

"I like watching you," I nibbled on the corner of my mouth as he sucked in a breath.

"You're killing me Baby," he muttered. "You come to me to protect you, and you want to watch me workout...do you have any idea what that means to me?"

I shook my head slowly as I watched him, "No."

"Working out is the last thing that I want to do now. All I can think about is taking you home and working out in private," he groaned right next to my ear.

"We can do that later," I giggled as I playfully smacked his rear.

He froze and grinned wickedly at me, "Watch it! I'm already holding on by a thread."

ooooooooo

Cole

"You two didn't fuck on my desk did you?" Wes smirked when Maddie and I rounded the corner smiling.

"Shut up!" I snapped "and don't talk like that in front of her."

"Sorry," Wes groaned as he held his hands up waving them in front of him. "You wanna go a couple of rounds?"

I turned to look at Maddie wanting confirmation that this was all right with her, but all she did was smile.

"I think the lady likes the idea of you getting your ass handed to you," Wes taunted.

"The lady likes the idea of him doing the handing," Maddie giggled. "Show me whatcha got," she rose on her tiptoes and pressed a kiss to my cheek.

"As you wish," I bowed enjoying our like a prince act as I offered her a chair, and moved to grab my gear. After strapping on my gloves, and slipping the mouth guard in place, I climbed through the ropes and bounced on my toes as I watched Wes roll his eyes at me.

"You better keep your head in the game this time," he popped his neck and wiggled his jaw. "I'm not going easy on you because your woman's here."

"Just shut up and punch me jackass," I lifted my gloved fists and knocked them against his.

"That can be arranged," he laughed as he reared back and took a swing at me.

oooooooooo

Maddie

After watching Cole and Wes go at it for at least an hour, we were finally leaving. I was tired, and as I climbed into Cole's Explorer, I yawned. When he'd seen how stressed I was, he'd convinced me to leave my car at McKay's. He'd told me we could come back tomorrow and get it, or he'd have Wes follow us in it. He knew the anxiety I'd been feeling had done a number on me, and as much as I didn't want to relinquish control, I'd agreed with him.

I had tomorrow off, and Wes was going to bring my car by then. Knowing that Cole was going to keep me safe, lifted the burden that I'd been carrying most of the night, and now I was slowly letting exhaustion overtake me.

"Hey, no sleeping yet," Cole nudged me as we turned into the parking lot of his building. It had only been a few hours since I'd been here, but it felt like a lifetime. "Let's get you upstairs and into something more comfortable."

"I don't have anything here...what would I change into?" I turned to glance at him. He had a smirk firmly in place as he snickered, "Exactly!"

"Cole!" I gasped.

"What?" he rolled his eyes before turning to face me completely. "You're beautiful," he lifted his arms. "Why is it so hard for you to think that I don't enjoy you naked?"

I could feel my face heating, and I began twisting my hands together in my lap. Cole grunted slightly as he shoved open his door and rounded the front appearing on my side before I had a chance to react.

"I guess..." I trailed off.

"What?" he reached for my hand to help me out and then tucked me into his side as he led me to the door. "What's going on in there?" he pointed to my head. "Tell me...please?"

"Richard always said I was a lousy girlfriend," I let the words fly out of my mouth without taking a breath. I avoided looking at him, worried at what I might see when I did.

He paused with his hand on the doorknob as he quickly shook his head, "That asshole didn't know what he was talking about." He quickly unlocked the door, and tugged me in behind him before pressing me into the wall, and covering me with his body. "You are the sexiest thing alive, and I thoroughly enjoyed myself last night. Don't you ever question your abilities when it comes to fucking. You're brilliant…you hear me. Fucking brilliant, and I want an encore right now."

As his lips pressed to mine in a deep kiss, his palms slid around my middle and dipped into the back out my scrub pants cupping my rear. He began kneading the soft flesh as he pulled me into him. "Oh god, I want you," he groaned as he broke the kiss. "Right now!" He yanked his hands out, and gripped my top in the process, tossing is over my head. Our mouths crashed back together before we both fumbled with each other's pants. He was wearing a pair of athletic shorts, and as soon as I loosened the drawstring, they easily slid over his hips. His erection sprung free pointing directly where it wanted to be, and I shivered in anticipation. "So beautiful," he murmured as his mouth moved to run across my throat. He rolled his hips forward, rubbing his cock through the wetness that was slowly leaking down my thigh. "And so ready," he growl as a finger pushed into me.

"Cole?" I whimpered. I didn't know when I'd become so needy, but being around him seemed to bring out that side of me.

"Are you on the pill?" he murmured as a second finger joined the assault.

It took me a minute to realize what he was asking. I'd been on birth control since I'd lost my virginity to Richard. He'd refused to wear condoms, and I had no intention of ever having a child with him.

I nodded slowly against his throat as he groaned. "I'm clean, I swear. I never go without, but with you I can't wait."

"It's ok," whispered as I reached up and cupped his jaw. "It's ok," my eyes made contact with his, this beautiful, damaged man. We were still in the living room of his apartment, right by the front door, and it looked as if we were doing this here. He muttered something unintelligible before lifting me, and slamming into me in one giant thrust.

"Ahhh!" I yelled out just as he groaned, "Oh fuck!"

"You ok?" he panted as he fought to hold onto his sanity.

I quickly nodded as I wrapped my arms around his shoulders, and leaned in next to his ear. "Better than ok," I nipped at his ear and rolled my hips.

"Awe shit," he ground his teeth together.

At that moment, I knew what it meant when someone used the expression that they 'unleashed a beast.' Cole's entire body began vibrating with tension as he held onto me. His hips began to piston as his mouth devoured mine.

I ran my hands up into his hair tangling my fingers in it as my thighs tightened around his waist. I could tell he was close, and I felt my insides begin to tighten around him as he began to move even faster.

"Maddie," he warned. "I'm about to come. Are you close?"

I nodded against his chest slightly embarrassed that he was asking me this. Richard had never cared, and I'd gotten used to not being considered in this matter. "Let go," he panted as he moved one of his hands between us and pressed to the one spot he knew would send me into oblivion. As if on cue, I shattered around him as every muscle in me tightened. Cole offered a few more thrusts before erupting on a deep groaned. His body went ridged as a tremor raced through him causing him to gasp for breath. "Don't ever underestimate your ability," he gasped. "That was amazing," he pressed a kiss to my forehead before releasing my legs and slowly letting me slide down until my feet touched the floor. We stood there pressed against one another for a minute just gathering our senses.

When I finally began to feel my legs again, he stepped back, and glanced down at where my pants were piled on the floor. He chuckled as he stepped the rest of the way out of his before running his gaze back up my body. "Come on," he reached for my hand as he began leading me to the bathroom. "I'll help you get cleaned up."

I blushed as I glanced down at the mess that covered my thighs. I'd never been so wanton, and as I stared at his beautiful naked ass, I found myself wanting him again. "Don't worry," he called over his shoulder as he caught me staring. "I can go all night with you."

I swallowed at his blatant comment before brazenly responding, "So can I."

To say that we exhausted each other that night would be an understatement. Cole and I spent the entire night learning each other's bodies. We tried every way we could think to pleasure one another, and by morning we were completely sated in every way imaginable. Cole and I had broken each other that night, but we had done it in the best way possible.

Chapter 20

Maddie

"Whatcha thinkin' about?" Cole brushed his fingers lightly across my forehead pushing my hair back in the process.

"Nothing…everything," I murmured as I moved my hair to cover the spot he'd just cleared. "I don't know…"

"What's wrong?" he propped himself up on his elbow and peered down at me. "Talk to me."

"I can't explain it," I sighed. "I'm happy…I am, but…I'm scared."

"Of what? Me?" he motioned to his chest as his eyes widened.

"No...yes...maybe," I rolled onto my side facing away from him as I tried to gather my thoughts. "It's just that things are going so fast, and I'm not sure how to deal with it all yet."

Cole rolled to his back and blew out a breath as he muttered, "I thought this was going somewhere."

"It is," I gasped as I turned to face him. I could feel the tears forming in my eyes, and I refused to cry. After yesterday and last night, my emotions were all over the place. "I'm just a little freaked out," I placed my hand on his bare chest and watched his face soften. "I mean...you're the first person I've let get close to me in years, and I'm in bed with you...naked," I smiled hoping to ease the tension between us.

"You sure are," he grinned back at me as he rolled onto his side to face me, "and I like it."

"I like it too," I confessed, "but I can't shake the feeling that someone's been following me. It's only happened a few times, but I know they're there."

Cole pushed himself to a sitting position and ran his fingers through his messy hair, "Have you seen them?"

"No," I slowly shook my head.

"Then how do you know?" he reached for me and tugged me closer to his side.

"It's a feeling really. I mean…I can't explain it, but something's not right," I murmured as I turned my face and buried my nose in his neck. "I'm sorry."

"Hey," he tipped my chin up to look at him, "there's nothing to be sorry about. If you say you know, then I believe you. Wanna hang out at the gym with me today?"

"I don't want to be in the way," I mumbled.

"You won't be," he smiled as he leaned in and pressed a kiss to my forehead. "Come on," he slid from the bed and tugged me by the hand. "We need to shower first."

I let him pull me along as we walked towards the bathroom, but I couldn't help the slight limp that I had.

"What's wrong?" Cole wrinkled his forehead as he watched me hobble along.

"I think you broke me," I tried with everything I had to keep a straight face, but as Cole smirked at me, I couldn't help but burst into giggles.

"Hmmm," he scratched his chin. "I guess that means I have to take at easy later."

"Later?" I squeaked.

"Yeah...later...when I fuck you on Wes's desk," his smirk went into a full on grin at that point.

"What?" I gasped.

"You heard me," he shrugged. "After he put that idea in my head yesterday I can't stop thinking about it."

At hearing his admission, all I could do was gasp as he pulled me the rest of the way into the bathroom. While Cole turned on the water to warm it, I sat perched on the counter watching. A sense of peace and what I would describe as happiness settled over me. The foreboding from the day before was pushed to the back of my mind as I let myself be swept up in the moment. As long as I had Cole nearby, I knew I didn't have anything to worry about.

oooooooooo

"Where have you been the last few days?" Jo marched into my office and flopped down on a chair in front of my desk.

"Out," I shrugged as I continued to stare at the file in front of me. I'd spent the last three days with Cole, and I was behind now at work.

"Out where?" Jo pushed. She knew something was up, and had left me alone for the past several weeks, but I think I'd finally pushed her to the end of her patience.

"What is it that you want to know?" I glanced up at her with an annoyed look.

"You've been coming in late, leaving early, and spending an awful lot of time at the gym...I just want to know why," she grinned as she leaned back in the chair and crossed her legs.

"I'm seeing someone," I lifted a shoulder as the admission fell from my lips.

"What?" Jo rocked forward and grabbed the file out of my hands forcing me to look up at her. "What do mean 'seeing someone'? As in a guy?" her mouth dropped open as she stared at me like I was someone she didn't recognize. I kinda was...I mean in all the time we'd known each other, I'd never dated anyone. "Who?" she commanded.

"I'm not doing this with you," I muttered as I reached for the folder trying to get it out of her death grip.

"I'm not giving this back until you tell me," she countered.

"Fine," I tossed my arms in the arm and leaned back in my own chair. "His name is Cole.

We've been dating for a couple of weeks. Happy?" I scowled.

"Very," she gave a quick jerk of her head as she tossed the file at me. "When can I meet him?"

"And why would I bring him around you?" I teased.

"Because I'm awesome, and already dating someone. I can give him the once over," she winked. "We're going to Vibe this weekend. Seeing that you blew me off the last time," she waved her hand in the air as she rose to stand, "you should come...and bring Cole."

"I don't know," I turned to glance out the window as I sighed.

"Why not?" Jo cocked her head to the side. "You seemed to have fun the last time."

"I did," I nodded as I fidgeted in my chair. "I'll think about it." I knew Cole would go if I asked him to. When I had mentioned going there to him last weekend, he'd readily agreed. I figured with the way he seemed so enamored with me, he'd probably do anything I asked.

"Well, when you decide, let me know. Ben is going too, and we'll figure out a time later in the week," she shrugged before turning to disappear out into the hallway.

A few minutes passed, and as I continued to stare at files time seemed to stand still. What I really wanted to be doing was hanging out a McKay's. Cole was working today, and the idea of watching him waltz around the gym in nothing but a pair of athletic shorts had me craving his presence.

"Hey Maddie," Jo called from the hallway.

"Yes?" I groaned. It seemed like she was going to bug me most of the day. "What is it?" I called as I placed my elbows on my desk, and let my head fall into my palms.

"Delivery," she smiled as she walked back into my office carrying a long white box. "Looks like flowers," she grinned. "I wonder who could have sent them."

I couldn't contain the excitement that bubbled up inside me. I felt like a giddy schoolgirl as I reached out the take the box from her. "I don't know," I giggled. It had to be from Cole, but I was surprised that he would send me something. He didn't seem like the type, but he'd been surprising me a lot lately.

"Gimme," I placed the box on my desk, and pulled gently on the ribbon to release the bow. I glanced up at Jo and bit my lip, "Do you mind?"

"Oh…sorry. You can tell me about it later," she shrugged and turned to leave my office as she called over her shoulder, "You're one lucky girl."

I knew I was lucky, but when I lifted the lid to the box, and peeled the tissue paper back, lucky was the last thing I felt. There nestled in the red tissue was a black rose. I gasped in horror as I lifted the notecard that was lying across the stem. With shaking fingers, I blinked a few times before trying to read it.

I know

I dropped the card back in the box and quickly shoved the lid on it. All I could think about was running. I had to get away. All the fears that I'd had when I first came home five years ago came rushing back. He was here. He was watching me, and was choosing now to try and come back into my life. Richard was the one who'd been following me…and this note just confirmed it.

Without even thinking about it, I grabbed my purse and jacket, and raced toward the front door. As I passed Hannah's office, I stopped, and made an excuse to leave. She seemed to accept it, and didn't question me as she nodded and told me to have a good day.

Once in my car, I grabbed my cell and texted Cole.

Me: Can't come over tonight. Not feeling well.

Cole: I'll come to your place then. I can bring you something.

Me: I'm fine. I'll just see tomorrow.

He didn't respond after that, and I hoped that he would accept my excuse and stay away. The last thing I wanted was for Cole to get messed up in my past. He had enough going on, and adding to his burdens was the last thing that I wanted to do.

When I reached my apartment that afternoon, I scurried inside, locked the door, and sank to the floor. The terror I'd been fighting to keep hidden rushed to the surface and erupted as I clutched my knees and held them to my chest. All the possibilities that I'd seen in the future with Cole began disappearing one-by-one as the memory of the black rose came to the forefront of my mind. How could I have been so foolish to think that Richard wouldn't ruin this for me? Everything good in my life had been tainted by him, and now he'd wrecked this too. I screamed as I flung my keys across the room and watched them crash to the floor. Anger, fear, and sadness engulfed me as I mourned the happiness that I was sure to lose. How could I ask Cole to help with this? After what I knew about his past. How could I take him back there? I couldn't...that was the answer. I was going to have to let him go.

Chapter 21

Cole

"Huh, that's weird," I muttered as I looked at my phone again.

"What?" Wes looked up from the papers he was shuffling around in front of him to stare at me.

"Maddie was supposed to come over tonight, and she's cancelling," I reached up to scratch my head as I clicked the screen off on my cell and shoved it back in my gym bag.

"Well..." Wes smirked, "with the way you two have been going at it, maybe she just needs a break."

"Real funny Jerk," I grumbled.

"Seriously though...if you're that worried, just go check on her after you finish here," he shrugged before sliding his chair back and standing. "I've got a client coming in, and then my evening is totally open. I'll be fine if you want to head out then."

"You sure?" I watched him round his desk and head towards the front door to meet whoever had an appointment with him.

"Yeah. It's no biggie. Really," he called over his shoulder.

"Thanks man," I sighed.

Something was not right, and the more I thought about that text, the more it bothered me. Maddie never blew me off anymore. We'd gotten passed that after our first date. Wes was right though. Maybe she did need a break. We'd spent every night over the past week together. I was either at her place, or she was at mine. I was beginning to wonder if we even knew how to be apart. I guess I was going to find out tonight.

ooooooooo

When I left the gym that evening, I couldn't help the feeling of dread that settled in the pit of my stomach. I didn't know where it was coming from, but something was off. The text that Maddie had sent was still lingering in my mind. She had said she wasn't feeling well. Maybe she really was sick? Maybe it was a woman thing, and she just didn't want to tell me? Maybe I was reading too much into this?

I slammed my hands on the steering wheel of my Explorer as I sat in the parking lot. I'd been trying to convince myself to go home for the last ten minutes. I knew if I did, and I'd just sit there in my empty apartment and worry.

Finally giving in, I called my sister. I hadn't talked to her since before Maddie, and I had started dating, but she was the only woman I felt could give me an honest answer.

"Hello?" Angela's soft voice came on the line.

"Hey Ang," I sighed.

"Cole, what's wrong?" I could hear a slight panic in her voice, and I felt bad that I was worrying her.

"Calm down! I'm fine," I reassured her. "I need to ask you something."

"Oooookaaay?" I'd caught her off guard, and I snickered lightly.

"I met someone," I started but was cut off abruptly.

"A woman? You met a woman?" she gasped.

"Yeah, I met a woman," I rolled my eyes. I knew this would happen. I knew as soon as she found out about Maddie I'd get the third degree. Now I was just waiting for the firing squad of questions that were sure to come out of her mouth in the next thirty seconds.

"When? Where? What's her name? When can I meet her?" her mouth was going so fast I could hardly get a word in edgewise. "Wait...how long have you been seeing her?"

"Breathe Ang," I chuckled.

"I'm sorry," she laughed. "It's just...it's been forever since you actually dated anyone. I wasn't sure if you'd ever settle down."

"Well, Maddie was kinda of a surprise," I smiled to myself as I thought about how hard I'd pursued her when we first met.

"So that's her name? Maddie?" Angela giggled. "Tell me more," she begged.

"We've been seeing each other for about a month. We ran into each other at several different spots, so I don't know where you'd say we met."

"And?" she pushed.

"And what?" I grumbled.

"When can I meet her?"

"I don't know. She doesn't know about what I did. I'm afraid I'm going to have to tell her if she meets you and Mom," I pressed my palm to my forehead and sighed.

"Cole," Angela paused as if she was trying to find the right words. "You have to tell her. She needs to know, and if she likes you…then she'll understand. You did what you had to do for me…for us."

"I know but…" I trailed off as I thought back to that night I finally stood up to my father.

"You have to be honest," Angela coaxed. "Does she know? About what Dad used to do? Have you told her?"

"Yeah," I swallowed. "Ang…she's been through it too. Her exe…he was one sick sonofabitch."

"Wow! Really?" Angela gasped.

"Yeah really…and if she finds out I told you…" I trailed off.

"I won't say anything, but Cole? You need to be honest if you really like this girl."

"I know," I swallowed. "I think I might love her," I mumbled.

"Wow…I never thought I'd hear that come out of your mouth," I could hear her shuffling around. "So…why'd you really call? I know that you don't make calls out of the blue. What's bothering you?"

"I think I screwed up," I muttered. "She sent me a text today and blew me off."

"And?" Angela waited for the rest.

"And nothing. She said she wasn't feeling well. I think it might be girl code for something else," I sighed as I waited for my sister to impart some female wisdom.

"Maybe it means exactly what it says. Sometimes we need a night off Cole. Sometimes we're just not sure how to tell our boyfriends that we need a break. We don't want to hurt your fragile egos," her voice had a sarcastic tinge to it, and I knew she was rolling her eyes at me.

"I don't know. I just have this weird feeling that something's wrong," I grunted.

"Well," she mumbled. "You have two options…you can do what she asked and stay away, or you can go over to wherever she is and check on her. Just be prepared to have a door shut in your face. She might not want you around right now, and you might end up picking a fight."

"Thanks...you're a big help," I grumbled.

"I'm just telling you how it is Big Brother," she laughed.

"Yeah, yeah," I mocked. "I gotta go."

"You're going over there, aren't you?" she teased.

"You know me so well," I chuckled. "I'll talk to later Ang. Thanks."

"For what?" she asked.

"For listening," I clicked the phone shut, and cranked the engine. I was going to go over to Maddie's and find out what the hell was going on.

oooooooooo

Maddie

I'm not sure how long I'd been sleeping, but the pounding on my door jarred me awake. I sat up in bed so fast that my head spun slightly. I had no idea who it could be, but as I climbed out of bed and made my way to the door visions of Richard being on the other side assailed me.

When I got to the door, I paused and took a deep breath before calling, "Who is it?"

"Cole!" his voice was muffled. "Are you ok?"

I shook my head slightly as I tried to steady my voice, "I'm fine."

"Can you open the door and tell me that?" he begged.

I knew that if I opened it, I'd lose what little control I had over my emotions at the moment. Cole would see right through the façade, and press me until I told him what was wrong. "I'm not feeling well. I don't want you to get sick," I lied.

"Maddie…" he paused and then I heard a slight thump as he let his head or fist, and I wasn't sure which, bump against the door. "I've had my tongue down your throat for the last four weeks. If I were going to get sick, I'd already be that way."

I closed my eyes and blew out a breath. He wasn't going to take my excuses, and other than opening the door, and I saw no other way to get out of this aside from ignoring him. "Fine," I huffed as I began turning locks and stepping back to crack the door.

"What the hell!" he gasped as he moved closer. "You've been crying." It was a statement, not a question. "Why?"

"I told you!" I growled. "I don't feel well," I ground my teeth together. I watched his forehead crease and the frown lines appear as I began to tear into him. I knew he wouldn't go willingly, and I felt horrible, but it was the only way. "You know not everything has to be about you! Maybe I'm just tried and want, I don't know," I tossed my arms in the air, "a little break. Did you ever think of that?"

He stepped back as if I'd slapped him. "You don't mean that."

"How would know? Have you ever asked me?" I moved to push the door shut, but Cole placed the toe of his shoe in the doorway blocking me.

"I'm not leaving here until you tell me what's wrong," he crossed his arms over his chest and narrowed his eyes at me. "This morning you were fine. What happened today to cause this?"

"Nothing," I grumbled.

"Stop lying to me!" he shouted as he leaned right into my face. He pushed the door open, and I stumbled back slightly gasping as I caught myself on the couch behind me.

Cole stood in the doorway with a look of horror on his face. "I'm sorry," he shook his head as he reached up and began tugging on his hair with both hands. "Oh god! I'm so sorry. I didn't mean it," he scrambled in my direction and kneeled down in front of me as he reached for my hands. "Maddie," he swallowed. "I didn't mean it. You have to believe me."

It took my brain a minute to process exactly what had happened, but when it did, I yanked my hands from his. "Get out!" I pointed towards the door. "Get away from me! I don't want you to touch me! Leave!" I was screaming at this point as I began backing towards my bedroom.

Cole rose to his feet and slowly coward away from me. The strong, confident man I was so used to seeing was slowly turning into the scared little boy that had only made a few scarce appearances since we'd met. "Maddie?" he begged. "Please? I didn't mean it," his eyes teared up as he watched me retreat into myself.

All the progress we'd made was slowly evaporating right before his eyes, and I could see him finally accept his fate. He turned and shuffled towards the door as I stood there hugging myself. He'd done the one thing he swore he'd never do...he'd hurt me. In a matter of a few seconds, a few unplanned actions, he'd taken all the trust we'd built and blown it to smithereens. He'd taken me, and put me back in the same place that I'd been fighting to escape from for years. He'd become the one thing he vowed never to be...his father.

Chapter 22

Cole

It had been two days since Maddie had thrown me out of her apartment. I'd spent most of the night that night apologizing to her door. I don't know if she was listening to me, but I was trying. Now, all I wanted to do was beat myself to a bloody pulp. As hard as I'd tried not to, I was turning into the one person I loathed...my dad. I swore when I got him out of my life all those years ago that I would do everything in my power to not become him, and now...that's exactly who I was. I'd shoved my way into her apartment, and caused her to trip backwards.

As much as it was an accident, I couldn't forget the look on her face. She stared right through me that night as she screamed at me to leave. I couldn't blame her. I would have reacted the same way, but the worst part...the worst part was I'd become her nightmare. It was tearing me up inside to think about how she saw me now. I'd been so worried about her finding out my secret that I'd turned into hers. That asshole, Richard, had been haunting her for years, and as soon as we had begun to turn the corner I put her right back there where it started. I knew I had to fix this, but I had no idea where even to begin.

oooooooooo

"Hey asshole? You actually going to work today, or do I need to hire someone else?" Wes called from across the gym.

"Bite me!" I grumbled back.

When I looked up, I noticed he was flipping me off so of course I did the mature thing and grabbed a roll of tape to throw it at him. He dodged it, grabbed his gloves, and came striding towards me.

"Come on," he motioned towards the ring. "You look like you need it."

"How would you know what I need?" I growled.

"Well let's see," he tapped his chin like he was thinking. "You've been walking around here like a lovesick teenager for the past two days. Maddie hasn't been by, and you look like you're ready to kill somebody if they look at you wrong. I'd say you need it more than ever right now."

"Fine," I grabbed the gloves he was holding out, and ripped my shirt over my head. I narrowed my eyes at Wes before warning him, "I'm not in the mood for your bullshit today. Clean fighting...that's what I want."

"Fine," he held his hands up. "I'm kinda scared of you right now anyway."

I glared at him waiting for him to explain further, but he didn't. Finally, I growled, "Why?"

"Because I haven't seen you this conflicted in years. The last time I saw you spiral out of control was when your..."

"Don't you fucking say it," I pointed a gloved hand at him. "Just don't!"

"I won't," he backed away from me slightly as his eyes darted towards to the ring. "Come on."

Once I made it over there, I stepped through the ropes, popped my neck a few times, and did a few stretches. I bounced on my toes before turning to knock gloves with Wes.

"You ready?" he bent his elbow, ready to jab. When I popped my mouth guard in and nodded he sobered his face and commanded, "Hit me!"

"What?" it came out slightly muffled.

"You need this…now hit me!" he pushed my shoulder and then stepped back to brace for my blow.

I pulled back, and then brought my fist forward slamming it into his side. He shook it off, and then held up his hands to halt me. I watched for a minute curious to what he was doing, and then understanding dawned on me when he grabbed a pad. He nodded that he was ready once again, and I opened up on him. Punch after punch I went for his middle and face. Each time he lifted the pads to block me. All the anger I'd been holding onto since the incident with Maddie came rushing to the surface, and as hard as I tried to hold on I just couldn't. I felt like a pussy as my throat began to constrict. My chest tightened, and the pain surfaced as it slowly began suffocating me. Wes kept taking my assault, and every punch he blocked I threw that much harder.

"Come on…let it out!" he barked at me as I grunted. Sweat poured down my back and face mixing with the tears I'd be fighting to keep at bay. It was as if I'd opened the floodgates, and now I couldn't stop.

"I hate you, you bastard. Why'd you do this to me? You were supposed to love me! You turned me into you!" I screamed around the guard finally spitting it out, leaning forward, and placing my gloved fists on my knees. "He did this," I panted. "It's his fault that this happened."

"What happened?" Wes came over and gently placed his hand on my heavy shoulder. "What happened with Maddie, Cole?"

I glanced up at him and squeezed my eyes shut, "I hurt her. I hurt her bad. I turned into the same asshole as her exe."

"What?" Wes shook his head and stood up straight. "I don't believe that."

"It's the truth. She won't even talk to me. It's been two days, and I can't get her to answer the door, or the phone. I don't know how to fix this," I sighed as I tossed the gloves to the side and reached for my water bottle.

"She's gonna be at Vibe tonight," came a quiet voice from behind us. Wes and I both jerked our heads in the direction of the voice to see Erin standing there twisting a piece of hair around one of her fingers.

"How do you know that?" I murmured.

"She told me...at a meeting...her friend, Jo, isn't letting her out of it. They think she needs to get out," Erin shrugged.

"Are you going with her?" I lifted my arm to wipe the sweat off my brow.

"I told her I would meet her there. I came to invite you," she pointed to Wes. "Wanna come with me?"

Wes glanced at me and then back at Erin.

"Don't stay home on my account," I grumbled.

"You sure?" his forehead wrinkled with concern.

"Yeah," I nodded.

"Sure, I'll go," Wes smiled at Erin then looked back at me, "What are you gonna do?"

"Oh, I'm going," I ground my teeth together. "I wanna talk to her, and this might be my only chance."

"Well, all right then," Wes grinned at me before slapping me on the back. "I'll see you later," he turned and strolled away leaving me standing there still coming down from my workout.

ooooooooo

Maddie

Cole: I'm so sorry

Cole: Please talk to me

Cole: Can we get past this?

Cole: I need to see you

Cole: Please?

I stared at my phone as the tears dripped down my face. What was I supposed to do? Cole had been calling me multiple times a day for the past two days. His voice messages had gone from anger to sad, to helpless, and now were bordering on pathetic. When I hadn't called him back, the texts had started up. Now, I was getting a text about every two hours or so as he begged me to talk to him. I knew I should hear him out. My heart kept telling me that what happened was an accident that he didn't mean it, that he really did care about me, but my brain kept replaying him shoving me as he forced his way into my apartment. All I could picture when I thought back to that night was Richard and how he used to do the same thing. He would bully his way in whenever I tried to keep him away, and I had the scars to prove it.

Now, here I was crying in my bathroom as I tried to get ready to go out for the night. Jo had insisted that I come with them. She'd said that she was tired of watching me mope, and demanded that I come with them tonight. I don't know what she thought she was going accomplish, but here I was trying to put a smile on my face.

Just as I reached for my face powder, my phone buzzed alerting me of a new text.

Erin: Wes said yes. Are you ok with that?

Its fine

I placed my phone back down by the bathroom sink as I began trying to cover the circles that had been under my eyes for the past several days. Between the unexpected flower delivery and what happened with Cole, I hadn't been sleeping much. I wasn't planning on trying to impress anyone tonight, but I did want to look like I should be among the living.

As I finished applying my lip gloss, I took one last glance at myself before retreating into my bedroom. I still needed to pick something to wear, and Jo was picking me up tonight. I had wanted to drive, but she'd insisted and now I was sure it was because I'd been trying to back out all day.

After standing in front of my closet for who knows how long, I finally decided on a pair of skinny jeans and a loose light blue top. The color made my eyes pop, and as I tugged the jeans up I couldn't help but remember the last time I wore them. It took me a minute to get past the memory as I stood in front of my mirror picking at a piece of invisible lint. I'd worn these same pants the night Cole, and I made love for the first time, and as I ran my hands down my thighs, I couldn't help the feeling that settled in my stomach.

"Get a grip Maddie. He shoved you," I scolded myself. "You can't be with someone like that. He's just like Richard. You were fooling yourself to think otherwise." I'd been muttering to myself for so long it was as if I was having a conversation with an imaginary friend.

Before I could sink any further into my thoughts, there was a knock on my door. I jumped slightly before I heard a muffled shout come through it, "Come on Maddie. You're not getting out of this. Open the damn door."

I sighed. It was Jo, and by the sound of it she and Ian had already started drinking. "I'm coming," I called as I grabbed my keys, ID, and a wad of cash, and stuffed them into my pocket. I took one last look at myself before releasing a deep breath, and turning to walk into the lion's den.

oooooooooo

"So you have to promise me one thing tonight," Jo grabbed me by the shoulders, and spun me to face her.

"What's that?" I rolled my eyes as I glanced at where Ian was standing behind her.

"You have to dance. I don't care if it's by yourself, or with a guy, but you have to dance," she swayed a little to the side showing the effects the alcohol was already having on her.

"Jo," I sighed as I squeezed my eyes shut. "You're lucky I came."

"You promised you would," she shrugged. "You're loyal if anything. I knew you'd come," she hiccupped before she started giggling. "Maybe you need to come more," she whisper-shouted to me before glancing back at where Ian was chuckling behind her. "I know I am," she winked at him before sidling up to him and wrapping her arms around his waist.

"Oh god," I groaned as I looked up at the sky. "How much has she had?" I narrowed my gaze on Ian before shaking my head.

"Enough," he shrugged before turning them to face the direction of the door.

"I'm not driving, so back off Mom," she tossed her hand in the air.

As we made our way to the front door, I couldn't help the uneasy feeling that settled over me. It was like sixth sense that I'd developed after being with Richard. Whenever something bad was coming, I seemed to be able to feel it.

When I reached the front of the line, I gave the bouncer my ID and cover fee. Jo smiled drunkenly at me as she looped one of her arms through mine and began pulling me after her. I assumed that we were heading for a table in the back just like last time, but what I was met with when I rounded the corner was something I was not prepared for.

Right as I stepped into the darkness of the club I crashed face first into a wall of muscle. I sucked in a breath, ready to apologize until I looked up and saw whose chest I'd just stumbled into. The dark eyes that peered down at me held a sadness, and the crinkle that usually appeared around his mouth was missing.

"Hi," he murmured as he leaned down next to my ear so I could hear him.

I recoiled immediately remembering what had happened in my apartment as I pushed off his chest and tried to flee. "I've gotta go," I called to Jo as she stood there staring at the exchange.

"No," Cole reached out and wrapped his hand around my bicep. He didn't squeeze hard enough to hurt me, but it was enough to stop my escape. "I just wanna talk. Please?" he begged. "Please…just listen. You don't have to say anything."

I stood there in shock as I let the words sink in. My heart was telling me to give him a chance. He looked as if he hadn't slept in days. His usual scruff was longer, and his hair was messier, and the normal sparkle that his eyes held was absent. He seemed to be as wrecked as I was. My brain, it was another story altogether, it was screaming at me to run. Run as fast as I could in the other direction.

"Please Maddie?" he tried again.

I nodded slowly as I glanced back at Ian, "I'll meet you guys at the table in a minute." After Ian had nodded his agreement, he turned and left, Jo only looked back at me once. I sucked in a breath before turning back to Cole, "Let's go somewhere in the back where it's quieter."

He nodded and reached for my hand to lead me through the crowd. As soon as his fingers made contact with mine, I recoiled as if he'd burnt me. I was willing to talk, but I was still upset over what had happened, and I wasn't ready to forgive him yet. He glanced back at me, shock written across his face at my actions. I slowly shook my head as I watched him accept my fear. He knew what he'd done, and as I watched his shoulder slump, I knew we'd just gone back to the beginning. I think he knew it too, and that made my heart break just a little more.

Chapter 23

Cole

I don't know what I thought was going to happen, but Maddie was pulling away from me like I was a stranger was not it. On one hand I understood why she did it, but on the other I thought we'd gotten past this. The realization that I was going to have to work that much harder to get her to forgive me was slowly sinking in when I led her down a dark hallway near the restrooms, and I turned to see her curling in on herself.

"I'm so sorry," I murmured as I shook my head. I really didn't know what to say. I'd planned out this conversation the entire ride here, but now that I had her in front of me my brain had stopped functioning.

"I know," she sighed as she backed further away from me.

"But?" I reached for her, but it only caused her to wrap her arms around her middle and glance away from me.

"I can't do this again..." she trailed off as she began to shake.

"Maddie," I stepped closer to her and reached out to cup her cheek. "I can't tell you how much I want to take the other night back, but..." I glanced around before stepping closer, "I'm not him." I felt her tremble harder, and I shook my head. "I love you," I felt my eyes well up, and I cursed myself for letting my emotions show.

"What?" she gasped and stepped back. Her back hit the wall, and she began shaking her head furiously from side-to-side, "You can't...you can't say that!"

"But it's true," I tilted my head to the side and bent my knees so I could stare directly into her eyes. "I've been fooling myself to think otherwise. I've never met anyone like you. I love you, Maddie."

"How am I supposed to believe that?" she swallowed as she let tears spill from her eyes. "He used to tell me the same thing."

"Oh Baby," I wrapped my arms around her, and when she didn't resist, I pulled her into my chest. "I'm not him. I swear I'm not him. I'll do anything to prove that to you. Please?" I murmured into her hair, "Just give me another chance."

She sniffed and wiped at her eyes before tilting her chin up so she could look at me, "I want to, but I don't know if I can."

"I don't know how anyone could hurt you," I trailed a finger down her jaw, and stopped when I met her lips. "You're so sweet and perfect," I watched her eyes flutter and decided to take my chances. I leaned forward and let my breath blow across her face as I whispered, "If you don't want me to kiss you, then tell me to stop." When she didn't make a move to resist me, I leaned in further and brushed my lips lightly across hers.

At that moment, that brief second, I felt her body tremble once again before going lax against mine. Her hands came up, and fisted my shirt as she pulled me impossibly closer. When I pressed my hips into hers, she gasped and opened to me. It was as if she'd struck a match. The sweet kiss soon deepened and turned into one laced with passion…a passion we'd been ignoring for the past two days. She'd been fighting to resist me, and I'd finally gotten past the walls she'd tried erecting. "Tell me you forgive me?" I begged as I slid a hand down her body, and clutched her rear through those sexy as hell jeans. "Tell me you want me like I want you."

"I do," she whimpered. "I think I love you too," she whispered against my mouth.

I froze when those words left her sweet lips. I'd been waiting to hear them, and now that I had I wanted to savor the moment. I broke the kiss, but didn't back up as I looked down into her sparkling eyes. "Did you mean that? That you love me?"

She nodded slowly as her lips pulled into a crooked smile, "I've been fighting it for a while. I was scared to admit it to myself, but yeah…I love you."

I chuckled as I leaned in and pressed a quick kiss to her forehead, "You wanna get out of here?" I stepped back and smiled at her. "There are about a million other things that I'd like to be doing than standing in the bathroom hallway at a night club, and I'd like some privacy to do them in."

Maddie's cheeks turned an adorable shade of red as she sucked her lip into her mouth and began biting it. She nodded quickly and glanced around. "I have to tell Jo I'm leaving, but yeah...I'd like that too."

"All right," I reached for her hand, and this time she took it willingly and threaded our fingers together.

After saying our goodbyes to her friends, I began leading us toward the front door of the club. She was trailing behind me, and if the club weren't so busy I probably would have noticed more that she'd stopped moving when we began to pass the bar. I turned around to see what had happened, and was met with a pair of angry green eyes.

"What the fuck are you doing with my girlfriend?" the man stabbed his index finger into my chest.

I furrowed my brow as I searched for Maddie. I didn't know who this guy was, and figured that he was just drunk. "What are you talking about?"

"I mean I've seen you...with her," he pointed beside me, and when I followed his hand, I saw Maddie turning a scary shade of white. "She's mine!" he growled as he moved closer to me, but instead he grabbed her.

"Listen buddy I don't know who you think you are, but this is my girlfriend," I rolled my eyes at him as I reached for her. Maddie began cowering and shaking her head as she broke his hold on her and backed away from both of us. I couldn't figure out what was happening, but then I heard it. It was a whispered confession, and with the loud music of the club I don't know how I heard it, but I did.

"Richard," Maddie gasped as she slowly backed up further.

I watched her shrink back as she moved to the side trying to get behind me. She was terrified, and there was so much going on around us that nobody was really paying attention to this guy.

"Listen," I growled. This guy was annoying me, and all I could think of was getting Maddie away from him. "You not supposed to be anywhere near her."

"Says who, asshole?" he sneered at me as he reached in his pocket.

I could feel Maddie behind me, and then I heard her, "Please Richard? Just leave me alone. I don't want to be with you anymore. We've been through this. I left a long time ago," she babbled on and then I felt her hand fist the back of my shirt. I was just about to turn around and leave this loser when I saw a flash of light out of the corner of my eye. Maddie gasped and then screamed, "No!" just as Richard began wielding a knife. Instinctively I threw my arms out to protect her, and began backing us away from him and in the direction of the door. I glanced towards the bar hoping to catch a bartender's attention, but they were swamped with customers the moment.

"Richard, please?" Maddie begged as I reached back and pushed her further away from the situation. Watching all of this unfold right before me put me right back in the kitchen of my childhood home. There I was, thirteen years old again and deciding to fight back. As Richard lunged at me, I leaned back out of the way before taking a swing at him.

By this point, we'd garnered some attention, and several bouncers were shoving their way through the crowd to get to us. Richard had stumbled back after my first blow but lunged forward. I didn't realize what had happened until I heard Maddie's blood curdling scream, "No!!!!"

I darted my eyes around as I watched everything in slow motion. The bouncers had reached us and were wrestling Richard to the floor. The music became muffled, and the lights seemed to fade in and out. When I looked around to find Maddie, she was on her knees some ten feet away from me crying with her head in her hands. I wasn't sure what was happening, but soon realized I was on my side on the ground. I lifted my hand to wipe my brow, and that's when I saw it...blood. It was all over my hand, and when I glanced down to where it had been resting, I notice a small pool forming under my side. As if the fast forward button had been pushed on the evening, I soon began fighting to stay in the present. Memories of my past flitted through my brain before a calm settled over me and realization set in. I'd saved her. Maddie was safe...and now I could let go...

The End

Cole and Maddie's story will continue in Saving Us- Coming Winter 2015

Other Works by H. D'Agostino

The Second Chances series-

Unbreak Me- book one

The Boy Next Door- book two

The One That Got Away- book three

Inside Out- A Second Chances Novella 3.5

Fallen From Grace- book four

The Family Next Door- book five

The Shattered Trilogy-

Shattered (Shattered #1)

Restored (Shattered #2)

Renewed (Shattered #3)

Destined (Shattered 0.5) Coming Fall 2014

Untitled (Shattered #4) Cam & Avery- coming winter 2015

Standalones- Privileged

The Witness series-

Being Nobody- coming fall 2014

Acknowledgements

I'm always worried that I'm going to leave someone out one of these times so if I miss anyone, I'm truly sorry.

There are so many people to thank, and as I continue on in this journey of becoming a writer, the list keeps growing. I've met so many wonderful readers, authors, and bloggers over the course of the past year that I can't even begin to name you all. Thank you from the bottom of my heart. Meeting you at signings and hearing from you on the various social media out there is just the boost my heart needs. I appreciate all of you, and I don't have the words to truly express that.

Thank you to my wonderful, supportive, awesome beta Shellie for all your hard work on this book. I know I make you want to throw your kindle sometimes, but you're always honest with me, and have just the right words to keep me going. You chime in at just the right moment and seem to know exactly when I just need to vent.

Thank you to all the bloggers who have supported me and pimped this book out. Posting teasers, joining blog tours, and spreading the word about Cole and Maddie. Twinisie Talk Book Reviews, Sweet and

Naughty Book Blog, M&D's Have You Read Book Blog, Eye Candy Bookstore, Book Boyfriend Hangover, Author Groupies, United Indie Book Blog, and so many others just to name a few.

Thank you to MJ Fields for hooking me up with an awesome new cover designer. It looks amazing. Thank you for all your help in making several new connections in the book world. I can't put into words how happy I am.

Thank you to Kathy Coopmans of Panty Dropping book blog for hooking me up with an awesome photographer and introducing me to Tessi, who is featured on my cover. Kelsey is an amazing photographer and thanks to you I now have a one of kind cover for this book.

Thank you to Everything Marie for hosting a kick ass blog tour to launch this book into the published world. It was everything I hoped for and more.

And finally...

Thank you to all the readers out there for loving my books and wanting to meet Maddie and Cole. I hope you loved them as much as I do, and I can't wait to share Saving Us with you.

About the Author

H. D'Agostino currently resides in Syracuse, NY with her husband, two children, two dogs, and three cats. Originally from Harrisburg, NC, she attended UNC Charlotte and received a BA in Elementary Education with a concentration in Math. Heather loves hearing from her fans. You may follow her on Facebook at www.facebook.com/H.DAgostino.Author

Or on her website H. D'Agostino- Books at

http://hdagostinobooks.weebly.com

Or on Twitter at

hdagostino001